Abebi

A FOOTBALL NOVEL

TEXI SMITH

Abebi

A FOOTBALL NOVEL

TEXI SMITH

First published in 2024 by Popcorn Press, an imprint of Fair Play Publishing

PO Box 4101, Balgowlah Heights, NSW 2093, Australia

www.popcornpress.com.au

ISBN: 978-1-923236-13-4

ISBN: 978-1-923236-14-1 (ePub)

© Texi Smith 2024

Cover design and typsetting by Ana Sečivanović

Front cover photograph by SeventyFour

All inquiries should be made to the Publisher via sales@fairplaypublishing.com.au

A catalogue record for this book is available from the National Library of Australia

Dedication

To the one and only Michelle

CONTENTS

Chapter 1

Holiday

"Get up 'Bebi."

"What's happening?" she murmured sleepily, squinting as the light of her dad Charles' keyring lit the room briefly.

"It's time," he said quietly. "Time to move."

Abebi could see her sister Yetunde's startled face behind her father as he scrambled around, looking for something under the mattress. He was cursing but gave out a long breath when he found what he was looking for: an envelope half sticking out of the floorboards, almost lost in the dirt beneath.

"Where's Mum?" asked Abebi.

"She's already outside," said Charles reassuringly. "Come on, we need to go."

They walked outside the hut. The once neat patch of dirt where Abebi had planted seeds and had watered meticulously over the last three weeks was trampled. A white delivery van sat waiting, its engine turned off. There was a flicker of light coming from another torch as Abebi's mum loaded their meagre belongings. Abebi fidgeted with her pocket to make sure her battered old football cards were still in there; Youri Djorkaeff and Jay-Jay Okocha were on this journey with her. The driver was standing having a cigarette, totally unconcerned at his passengers' efforts at lifting the bags into the van. Charles raced over to help his wife, Adenike. He beckoned the girls in and they sat on a pile of soft bags. The driver casually finished his cigarette and appeared at the open back doors of the van. He stared at Charles, raising his eyebrow.

"Yes, of course," said Charles, reaching into his pocket and pulling out a few of the bank notes that were in the envelope. He handed the notes to the driver, who counted them and shuffled them into a neat pile. It looked as though he was contemplating something before folding them and putting them in his own pocket. He then lifted some of the other soft bags on top of the family, making sure there were enough on top so they couldn't be seen.

"When we are at the border, stay down," said the driver, a lot more friendly now that he had his money.

They drove off, the family in the back and the driver listening to the inane chatter of his radio that was tuned in to what sounded like a football match. They couldn't see anything out of the windows except for the lights of oncoming cars as they passed, and then an extended period of illumination as the van stopped and the driver had a jovial conversation with someone. Abebi had looked at her mum holding Yetunde tightly, her mum's eyes wide open and focused while her sister slept in her arms. Abebi could feel her own beating heart against her shirt and hoped no one could hear it.

"We're in Papua now," shouted the driver as they moved on, sounding upbeat.

Charles reached over and grabbed Adenike's hand. They had reached the next country on their quest, but they knew this one could be the most dangerous yet. There was still a long way to travel and the driver would only take them so far. Abebi was aware of their goal; her mother had talked about Australia a lot in the past and this three-month journey to a new life had been sold to the kids as a holiday. They had sold their house in Zambia where the kids had lived all their lives. The political situation and an influx of Rwandan refugees had heightened tensions, and Charles had been subjected to a lot of abuse himself for being an alien from another country. Both Charles and Adenike were originally from Senegal and had moved to Zambia some years before, but they had been tarred with the same brush as all other immigrants, and life had become increasingly difficult.

The holiday idea sounded feasible to Abebi. They had caught a flight from the capital, Lusaka, and touched down in Kuala Lumpur, where the heat and humidity were unbelievable. They had even spent their first night in a cute hotel room before starting an epic journey via land and sea through Malaysia and Indonesia. Along the way they had battled sickness due to the heat and were easy targets for looters, until they arrived on the island of Papua. Charles found work in Kota Jayapura, helping a local cobbler, while they worked out their next move, and the rudimentary hut that they lived in became a home for almost a month. All the while, Charles was plotting the final leg of the journey, perhaps the most treacherous, through Papua New Guinea and on to Australia.

Abebi and Yetunde still completely believed that they were on holiday, and their mum kept a bright and cheery disposition despite being far away from what she knew. Now they were in the back of a van, hiding under laundry bags and hurtling along a bumpy road through wildest Papua New Guinea. Abebi was starting to have doubts.

"Where are we going?" she asked her mum.

"Oh, my love," said Adenike. "We're going to a magical place where we'll have the best of everything."

"Why are we in a van covered in bags?" she asked.

"We're travelling economy class," said Adenike with a smile.

Charles hushed them, and they travelled in silence, drifting to sleep.

Chapter 2

Wanderer

The journey to the city of Lae had taken three days, including stopping in a town called Madang where they had joined another four African families for a festive evening and driven the last leg in convoy. The laundry van had become a truck carrying fruit, and by the time they arrived in the new city, they had upgraded to a minibus. The danger of being caught and turned away back to Indonesia was non-existent, and they could have been a group of international students or hospital workers, not worthy of a second glance from the police who passed them on the twisting highway.

Despite the long distances and the unusual modes of transport, Abebi still had no reason to doubt her parents, and she and Yetunde were enjoying being able to see out of the windows on this latest leg of their holiday. They pulled into a campsite on the edge of town, a properly run camp with a reception and a fence around it, and there were tents set up ready for the families to move straight in. The girls squealed with delight when they saw they had beds inside, all made up with linen, and they jumped around excitedly waiting to show their mum. This was living!

The day was turning into evening, and a group of what was clearly the dominant African population in the camp started to assemble on the lush green patch surrounded on three sides by trees. Makeshift goals had been erected, made from long straight branches of what looked like the most abundant tree in the area, and a fishing net was draped over the goals and shaped into a proper goal net using pegs and string. The families who had just arrived were invited over, and a barbecue started up. Clearly, this was going to be dinner, too, and everyone in the camp seemed to want to be there. Two teams were forming; a referee, dressed in full referee kit, summoned two captains for a toss of a coin, and the winning captain took a bag of shirts and started to distribute them to his teammates. There were two women on the team who had no qualms about taking off their shirts and putting on the playing shirt.

Abebi stared in disbelief at the off-white shirts from her position close to the sideline. She could see that the badge read BWFC in those strange-looking letters and she knew straight away it was her beloved Bolton Wanderers. Abebi had been mesmerised by reruns of the club's time in the English Premier League on TV back in Zambia; they weren't very good, but they always seemed to have an older superstar or ex-international in their team who did all the flicks and tricks. Abebi loved football, but hadn't been old enough back home to join in with the boys at school.

The crowd grew as the game wore on, and the blend of skill and flair mixed with incredible bravery and a no-holds-barred approach to tackling made this quite the spectacle. The non-white side playing in 'skins' took the lead with an intricately constructed goal from a breakaway, Bolton Wanderers equalised with a full-length diving header and the 40-minute game went to penalties. The goalkeeper for Bolton, one of the two girls, pulled off an amazing save to win the game, and the players of both teams rejoiced as if they had won the FA Cup. Abebi was transfixed, and she made her mind up that she was a Bolton Wanderers fan for life right there and then.

She was handed a flatbread filled with barbecued vegetables and devoured it. The smoky taste of the sweet capsicums and pumpkin left her craving more, but she had left it too late, and there was none; she'd be hungry again in two hours, but that would be nothing new.

They were settling in for the night, the flicker of a keyring light from Mum's bed the only light in the tent. Charles bundled into the tent, his foot trapped in the door flap and almost tripping him up, before having a quiet conversation with Adenike. They both then sprang to their feet and a light went on in the tent.

"We're moving again," said Adenike to the girls, who were both wide awake in the bed they were sharing.

"Awww," said Abebi, who was already feeling like she'd found a place to call home.

"This is exciting!" said Adenike, with no hint of excitement, and she busied herself with packing the few items that had been unpacked back into their bags. "Make sure you check under your bed and in the sheets for any clothes."

The two girls dutifully searched under the bed and through the sheets and found nothing. The football cards were still in Abebi's pocket; she felt the outline just to make sure. Adenike made the beds quickly and straightened everything back to the way it was earlier in the day. Charles held Yetunde's hand as they walked into the night with their bags, Adenike and Abebi carrying the bulk of their possessions as they followed behind.

They walked across the football field and through the trees to a road that ran alongside the river. There was another white van, the ubiquitous vehicle driven by every business person in Papua New Guinea, with its engine on but lights off. The driver was rolling a cigarette and continued to roll it while the family took their place in the back of the van, this time behind some crates of fruit and vegetables. Abebi watched as her dad passed on another note from his envelope. It was beginning to look a lot easier to fold to put back in his pocket.

The journey started on a lovely, smooth road. Through the front window, they could see the signs for what looked like a National Park, and the road suddenly became very different. The 100 km/h speed was reduced to less than 50, and there were plenty of twists and turns. The tutting of the driver at one point suggested that there might be an issue with the van, but he was negotiating with a local in a remote outpost and came into the back and took out a few trays of strong-smelling red fruit that didn't return. The rest of the journey was the same, with day breaking and a number of stops where a similar negotiation took place. The steep uphill had become an equally steep downhill and there was a chill in the air that whistled through the back of the van that had shed most of its produce.

Chapter 3

Hector

The family had miraculously managed to get some sleep, and they were woken as they came to a stop by the sounds of the sea, a busy port bustling with business. Abebi guessed that the driver would spend the day here loading up new cargo to take back up the mountains, but she wasn't sure that anyone would be taking their place behind the crates. This was surely a one-way journey. The driver shouted out of his window and a friendly-looking man appeared at the side and peered in to see what was in the back.

"Hello, my friends," he shouted in English. "You are looking for Hector?"

"Yes, Hector," replied Charles, immediately alert and smiling from ear to ear at the sound of a name that he was hoping to hear. Adenike squealed like she did when she was laughing along with friends.

The footsteps went around to the back of the van, and the doors were opened.

"Come!" said the man. He smiled and held out his hand to Charles, who took it for a handshake and a steadying hand down out onto the pavement.

"We are ready to leave now that you are here," said the man. "Hector is waiting in the boat, come!"

They slowly gathered their belongings and stretched their weary legs. Yetunde tugged at her mum's skirt; she had to go to the bathroom and was already in the squat position. Adenike picked her up and took her to the side of the pavement and a jet was already streaming into the gutter by the time she had put her down. Abebi didn't want to go in front of everyone and held hers in. They had purposely not been drinking much to avoid having to stop, and now Charles handed the bottle to Abebi, who gulped down the last of the water.

They were led along a long pier to a waiting fishing boat. No one seemed too interested that four African people were getting into a boat, and it was no surprise to see another 20 or so similarly black heads looking in their direction when they stepped on board. The man, who was obviously Hector, the captain of the boat, stuck his head out of the cabin window.

"Welcome aboard," he said cheerily before making the international sign for money by rubbing his thumb across his first two fingers. Charles dropped his bags, trotted over to the window, and shook Hector's hand. He handed over some notes and was prompted to hand over another, Hector's finger pointing at all four of them as if to say that it was a little more for all of them. The boat indeed had been waiting for them and the man who had met them unlooped the rope and threw it on the deck. Captain Hector gave a toot of his horn and a wave and they were off to sea.

"You know where we're going?" asked Charles to the man sitting next to him with his daughter in his arms, who looked as though he may speak English or French.

The man smiled. "We're going to Australia," he said.

"Do you know where we will land?" asked Charles.

"There is an island along the coast that is part of Australia," said the man. "I think we arrive there and then we can find our way to the mainland."

Charles smiled. He knew exactly where they were going, but was simply making conversation. He knew that Saibai Island indeed was part of Australia, but that there was no chance of seeking asylum there, and Charles' final contact, arranged all those weeks ago back in Zambia, would be the final piece in a multi-legged itinerary that had taken months to source.

"Do you have a boat to the mainland?" asked Charles, trying not to give away too much about his own plans.

"We're transferring straight from this boat on to the next," said the man, who finally held out his hand. "Edouard is my name. You are?"

"Pleased to meet you, Edouard," said Charles. "Sounds like we'll be on the whole journey with you."

Abebi and Yetunde were enjoying the ride. There was water for everyone. There was a working bathroom and, as far as the girls were concerned, this was a lovely boat ride along the coast, seeing the sights of whichever country they were in. They saw smaller fishing boats casting their nets, they passed close to a village where boxes were thrown onto a motorboat that turned and sped back ashore. The water was calm and there was no hint of sea sickness. The sun was lovely and warm and the occasional spray from the edge of the boat was refreshing. Best holiday ever!

Abebi eventually started to wander and found a young boy wearing a football shirt. She asked him what shirt it was, but when he didn't understand, she gently straightened the badge and read it as Paris St Germain. A thumbs up was all she could do, and the boy gave a big grin, his front teeth missing. Abebi trotted back to where her mum was sitting with Yetunde fast asleep in her arm, and pulled out a shirt from her bag and put it on over her dress. It was still a little oversized, but it was a Liverpool shirt, and she skipped back to where the boy was sitting, hoping he would recognise it. She sat opposite him on the deck, tugged at the Liverpool badge and kissed it. The two of them laughed. The boy rolled a small football to her and she stopped it with her left foot. Still sitting on her bottom, she swapped to her other foot and rolled it back. The boy instantly knew what to do, and put out his foot to stop it and did the same thing. This went on for two minutes before the boy eventually kicked the ball in the wrong direction and had to quickly stand up and race to stop it from bouncing down the steps into the main part of the boat.

Captain Hector sounded the horn sharply and yelled "Down!" from the window. There were two other crew members who instructed everyone to get down on the deck and stay low. Everyone complied. The crew members moved some netting, making out that they were arranging to drop their net in to start fishing. Abebi didn't dare look up, but she could see the captain waving at someone in acknowledgement before resting back against his seat in relief. Abebi could see her mum and Yetunde, and there was a look of terror in their eyes.

Abebi gave a thumbs up after seeing the captain relax, and in another two minutes, Hector hollered "Okay!" from the window and waved his hand to say they could get up. The crew members moved the netting back and disappeared below deck. There were no boats to be seen, but they had obviously just missed an encounter with someone who might ask questions about why there were 20 African people on board a PNG-registered fishing boat heading along the coast.

The sun was getting low as they finally came into calmer waters, and the boat moored at a rickety jetty next to the main wharf, which had a ferry unloading vehicles laden with produce. Again, it was busy, and again, there was no one concerned that the jetty was suddenly filled with 20 or so strikingly different-looking people and their belongings. A second, much smaller boat was waiting, and Hector reversed it back out while the fishing boat chugged into shore, where it was moored to a metal bollard. The smaller boat came up alongside, and they all looked inside and then at each other. There were raised eyebrows. This made the fishing boat look like a five-star cruiser.

"No problem, no problem," said Hector, who had walked back onto the fishing boat and was now starting to load up the travel-weary and unsure passengers. There was room, with a handful of the passengers having made their way ashore, obviously with other plans. There wasn't much space, though, once they had all moved across, and with the extra cargo of white polystyrene boxes of seafood, the smell and the attention from the birds would take a bit of getting used to. Charles and Adenike were still cheery, though. There was a small table that had water, fruit, and bread, which distracted everyone as they were pushed back from the jetty, and the engine roared to life with a plume of black smoke. Charles and Adenike looked at each other again with wide eyes before Charles shrugged and they continued to pass the food around their fellow passengers.

Chapter 4

Economy

Night had fallen, and the remaining passengers started to try to find a comfortable spot for sleep. Abebi and Yetunde were already fast asleep, their parents acknowledging that there was no chance of getting horizontal themselves.

"Heh heh, definitely economy class, this leg," laughed Charles, and Adenike gave him a narrow-eyed stare before chuckling along with him.

The water was still very calm, but an abrupt end to the constant humming of the engine brought the adults in the group back to life, and the two crew members made their way below deck to see what the issue was. There were a few tries at getting the engine back up and running and a constant stream of babble on the radio. This didn't look good. Abebi had just woken to hear another boat come close, and an additional crew member joined the boat, wearing oil-stained dungarees and carrying equipment. There was banging, some turning of the engine that didn't result in the engine starting, before two of the three men left the boat, and the third went to radio for a final time.

Charles got up as the third man went to board the other boat and pulled him by the arm.

"Where are you going?" asked Charles.

"Engine repair in the morning. We come back when light," said the man before politely shaking off Charles' grip and jumping into the speedboat.

Charles turned to see seven or eight sets of worried eyes staring in his direction.

They watched as the speedboat turned and disappeared from view, the flickering light bouncing gently up and down until it was gone.

Charles looked at Edouard and beckoned him to follow him down into the bowels of the boat. They crouched down and crept through into the area where the engine was sitting idle. The cover was off, and there was a heavy smell of oil. There was a light that Edouard turned on, and they could see that the area was a real mess. Some footsteps saw the appearance of a broad-shouldered middle-aged lady who nodded in the direction of the engine. Charles and Edouard stood back, and she knelt on the floor.

"Oh my," she said after barely 10 seconds. "Are there any oil containers around here? This oil is like Mama's soup!"

She raised her fingers that were covered in oil, and indeed, it was full of thick globules.

"We need some new oil," she said, wiping her hand on a rag that had very few non-black patches of material. She introduced herself as Aicha, an engineer from Chad who also worked as a car mechanic in her neighbourhood on the weekends. They scoped the area. There was a stack of small oil containers, like the ones a bulk buy of olive oil might come in, and Edouard pointed Aicha to it for further inspection. She picked up a few empty ones and put them to one side and finally came across a full container that still had a seal.

Dragging two of them across the floor, she put them next to the engine.

"I should really save the old oil," she said. "But look at this place, oh my god!"

She opened up a screw after finding the right tool for the job, and oil started oozing slowly across the floor. They all looked at each other.

Aicha threw the rag on the floor to divert the flow of the oil so their feet wouldn't get covered. She unscrewed a second screw, and the oil glugged out faster. It kept coming, so Aicha fashioned a funnel from the remnants of a cardboard box, making sure the smooth side was inside the funnel.

They waited for what seemed like half an hour but may have only been five minutes. The oil was only dripping now, but the pool on the floor continued to grow. Charles made a barrier of rags to keep the oil away from the engine. Edouard went back up on deck to let the others know what was happening.

With the first screw now secured and the funnel wedged in place, Charles lifted the first oil container as Aicha caressed the funnel to stop it from crumpling under the weight of the heavy liquid. They remained in place, topping up the funnel and making sure that the oil was still flowing into the engine. Edouard took over from Charles, who was starting to wobble under the strain, and they remained in position until three containers had been emptied.

"That should do it," said Aicha, screwing the screw back in as Edouard put the container on the ground and flexed his aching bicep. "Now we turn the engine manually, and then we try to start it."

Charles had no idea what that meant and left her and Edouard to it, heading back up on deck to get some fresh air. Adenike remarked that he smelled so bad and that he had been gone for ages. The boat was clearly not anchored and was floating aimlessly with the current. It was unlikely that they'd see their crew members return at all.

Some banging and then some whining signalled the first attempt at starting the engine, and it sounded promising. There was light as the sun was getting ready to appear, and the engine again whined before bursting into life with a huge roar. Everyone on deck cheered. The roar subsided to a hum, and Edouard appeared on deck and presented

Aicha to everyone. There was a round of applause. They headed to the cabin to work out the controls, to decipher the maps and to try to work out their position, but they were sadly lacking in knowledge. Debate about the position of the sunrise suggested that they should head south; after all, mainland Australia was barely 100 kilometres away, and they would make that in no time. What they didn't know, though, was how far they had drifted on the currents and in which direction.

The general consensus was to head south, and with the sun now providing a beacon for where east was, they headed forward with the sun on their left to what they hoped would be their ultimate destination.

Edouard remained in the cabin as Aicha and Charles joined the rest of the passengers on deck. Charles reached into his bag, grabbed a fresh shirt and quickly changed his oily t-shirt. He lifted some water from the ocean using a bucket and dunked the t-shirt in it, swishing it around. He tipped the oily residue from the top of the bucket and went to fill the bucket again. The t-shirt was washed out of the bucket as he did so and that was the last he saw of it as it quickly disappeared behind the boat. He smiled. What an idiot! Abebi was watching over the side and saw it all unfold.

"You really didn't want that shirt, did you?" she said, smiling.

"No 'Bebi," he said, grinning back. "Memories of our old life."

Chapter 5

Australia

The radio crackled from time to time, but there was nothing that anyone could understand. The afternoon sun was quite fierce now and everyone was trying their best to be covered. They had seen no one and there was no sign of land all day. Charles had been assumed as the de facto head of the passengers, and he spent the day recording the names of the passengers with Abebi and getting to know a little bit about them.

Aicha was with her sister and they had enjoyed a similar experience to Charles and his family; they were hoping to start a new life anywhere in Australia. Edouard was with his wife and baby and he had been forced out of his country due to a civil war and used his savings to fly to Indonesia as a tourist and then chance a similar journey from there. There were three teenage boys who had been drafted into a conflict between Eritrea and Djibouti and who had escaped from Eritrea and gone on an amazing journey by plane, boat and motorbike to arrive at the port in PNG. Two families of four made up the group, and contrary to initial headcounts, there were 20 of them.

The arrival of sea birds to the boat gave cause for optimism and a passing container ship in the distance suggested that they may be approaching land. The maps suggested Cape York at the northern tip of the Queensland mainland, but they had been travelling for so long without sighting any islands that Charles and Edouard discussed they may be further to the west and heading for the Northern Territory.

They weren't going to get much further though, the engine finally running out of fuel and the boat drifting aimlessly just as they spotted land. Aicha found a small can of what she hoped was fuel and they limped towards the land, almost beaching themselves on a small island before managing to push the boat off with some long planks of wood and they floated in to a wide sandy beach and became lodged in the sand.

The markings on the sand suggested that there was some wildlife that they might not want to encounter, a slithery path with footprints either side signalling the high possibility of crocodiles in the area. They had seen some big fish on approach, and they could have been sharks. This was not going to be a place to camp or to sleep or to cook. The three Eritrean soldiers pulled the boat as far into the sand as they could as the tide retreated, and the boat listed to the side and was effectively beached. Charles suggested that they might want to look for people, as they could see a red dirt road at the north end of the beach. Charles talked himself into going, and enlisted Aicha and her sister Zara to provide the softer touch if they did come across anyone. The three soldiers ventured into the trees by the side of the beach to see what they could find.

The dirt road had recently-made tyre marks and after only 500 metres they saw a road leading off to a property in the distance. The chances of them landing on a deserted beach right next to a farm were so small that Charles joked with the ladies that this could be a mirage. The red dirt blew in the air as they walked. They approached the building that looked like a collection of temporary cabins joined together to form a big house. They were greeted by a barking dog who bounced around them excitedly, and that attracted the attention of whoever lived in the property. A door swung open in the distance and a man with a shotgun appeared on the front verandah.

Chapter 6

Nhulunbuy

"Mr Williams, you have been so kind to us," said Charles.

After arriving on the shores of the Gove Peninsula, about 10 kilometres from the remote Northern Territory town of Nhulunbuy, and taking a chance on the first property they reached, the group of 20 were so delighted to have a cool, dry place to sleep the night. Charles had approached the gun-toting Trent Williams without any fear and Trent's gun leaned against the wall of the house within 30 seconds. Charles had always had a way with words, and his years running a shoe sales and repair store back in Zambia had given him all the small talk he would ever need. This was different, though, and he was perhaps lucky that Trent was easily won over.

Charles explained that they had a fishing boat that they would like to trade for a few nights' accommodation. It was a big call. Who would have space for 20 people, and who would want to buy a rickety old fishing boat with an engine swimming in oil? After riding Trent's tractor back to the beach and Trent having a look at it, the deal had been made and the fishing boat dragged through the bush to the property. The old converted barn, where backpackers would come and help tend to the vast complex of covered garden that used to flourish in the area, was perfect—it had beds for at least 10 of them, and enough spare mattresses to give everyone a comfortable spot to recover from the arduous days at sea and the weeks of travel that preceded it. It had two bathrooms and a rudimentary kitchen. The market garden was no longer operational. The covers were ripped from one too many storms and the raised soil beds were weathered by the wind and sun.

Trent couldn't believe his luck. He had been thinking about resurrecting the market garden after being offered a grant to supply the local shops with his produce to avoid the shortages of food they had every year during the wet season, and was at the point of picking up the phone to start searching for hands to help out. He would provide fresh food for the group, and in return they would help him restore the market garden to its previous working state. He had all the equipment and went on a mission with his big truck and trailer to the hardware store for all the essential parts to help restore life into his since dormant business.

"I need to thank you," said Trent. "You turned up in that tiny boat at just the right time. You can't stay here forever though. They're already talking in town. Word travels fast around here."

"We will stay here as long as you need us," said Charles. "Everyone here has a place to get to, and we might need some help getting there. For now though, we're happy to help you here."

Chapter 7

Police

The mutual understanding between Trent and his guests was shattered though on the eighth day. The three Eritrean soldiers, who had worked like machines since they arrived, had found a key under a stone in the basement of the barn, which they tried in a few of the locked doors until they hit the jackpot. They found three crates of NT draught, perhaps 20 years past their best-before date, and decided there and then that they would celebrate their first week in Australia with a round of heritage beers. The three of them raced upstairs as dinner was being cleared away and bolted through the door laughing. They started up the tractor and drove along the track to the road and off on a precarious adventure. By the time Trent had found the keys to his truck and made off after them, there was a trail of destruction. A Ute that was parked up and marked For Sale was smashed into and the tractor had veered down the side of the road and into a ditch and rolled on its side. Trent's wife Margot had called the police and they arrived at the scene as Trent did, the three soldiers still laughing at their escapades and making no sense at all.

Trent convinced the two policemen that they should come back in the morning and assess the situation, and they all helped to turn the tractor back on its wheels and backed it up onto the road with the help of a rope tied to the police car.

Trent, Charles and Aicha sat the three boys down when they were dropped off by the police.

"You know what's going to happen tomorrow?" said Trent.

The boys were silent. Charles and Aicha looked at Trent.

"The police are going to come here and take everyone away," he continued. "And look, that's probably going to get you to where you want to be a little quicker anyway, but I'm so sorry that your stay here has to end this way."

Charles had a tear in his eye. Aicha was staring at the three miscreants as if she was going to rip into them at any moment. They sat with their heads bowed, only looking up occasionally. The vintage beer had started to wear off and the hangover was coming.

"Thank you for everything, Mr Williams," said Charles, standing up and shaking Trent's hand. "I too am sorry that we have to leave this way, but thank you for giving us time to pack up and be ready."

Trent stood up and hugged Charles and Aicha. He gave each of the boys a light slap across the head and a smile as he walked past on his way to the main house and to bed.

Abebi knew something was up when they woke. Everyone was still in the room, and the grown-ups were packing bags.

"Mum, what's happening?" she asked. Adenike held out her hand, and Abebi held it.

"It's time to go on our next adventure," she reassured.

Two hours later they loaded a school bus with their belongings, each of the 20 in the group saying a farewell to Mr Williams. They endured a bumpy start to a 25-minute drive along a straight road before arriving at Nhulunbuy Police Station and unloading the bus. There was minimal security. The officer in charge simply counted heads on a number of occasions as each of the families and then the individuals were processed in a big room. Once each party had been processed, Charles acting as the unofficial translator, they moved from one side of the room to the other. Most of the group had passports of varying colours, but Edouard didn't have one for his baby daughter and two of the soldiers had passports that had expired. The other said he had never had one, which made it even more amazing that he had made it this far. Charles kept a record of each of their names. He carefully took down mobile phone numbers and email addresses, even though they didn't have a working mobile device between them.

Charles asked the policeman in charge if he could use a computer, and he was handed an open laptop, one of those rugged unbreakable machines that was quite bulky. He stared at it in wonder. The others looked at him as though Charles wouldn't know what to do. He did though, and could see that the laptop was connected to the internet. He quickly opened a browser and logged in to his email using his Hotmail account and started to type in the details he'd taken down, comparing them to the list he'd previously made on the boat, in a new message before sending it to himself. He had hundreds of emails, many from concerned family in Senegal and friends in Zambia, but wasn't going to start replying to them all. He glanced at Adenike and then decided he should send a message to her sister, a quick one-liner to say that they were safe and well in Australia. He logged out and walked over to Aicha.

"Do you need to contact anyone?" he asked.

"Do you have a phone?" she asked.

"No, but we can send emails," said Charles.

"I've never sent an email," she replied.

Charles asked the rest of the group and it was only one of the soldiers, the one without the passport, who knew anything about computers. Charles watched as he logged in to what looked like a government website and started to filter through emails and notifications. Charles caught his eye. The soldier smiled and looked back at the screen, typing furiously. Not so stupid now …

Everyone was now processed, and Charles was briefed about what would happen next. In a surprisingly efficient operation, they were booked on a flight from nearby Gove East Arnhem Airport to Darwin on the afternoon flight, where they would be taken to a 'processing' centre and from there they would be moved to appropriate accommodation. The lack of passports wasn't a problem, and they would be travelling with two police officers, one of whom was from Darwin and was keen to visit family. Charles was amazed at how friendly everyone was; he knew that Australia was the country of opportunity, the lucky country, a place where all nationalities lived together harmoniously, but he had expected to be arguing and shouting at this stage of the journey and had prepared himself for such a situation. Charles thanked the police officers and relayed the information to Aicha and Edouard so they could pass on the details in the relevant languages to the rest of the group.

Charles took a seat next to Abebi and Yetunde and grabbed them both, hugging them tightly. The two girls giggled, loving the attention of their father. This fantastic holiday was moving on to the next leg and they were excited. Charles took them by the hand over to the wall near the front desk where there was a map of the Northern Territory. It was a huge slice of Australia with dead straight borders and a bulging coastline. He pointed out where they were and where they were going. They were heading west from one side of the state to the other. Charles was absorbed in the map and the girls had lost interest and were looking at pictures of crocodiles on the lower part of the wall.

Chapter 8

Darwin

By the end of the day, the whole group had been taken to the airport, enjoyed an hour-long flight with drinks and snacks, boarded a bus on arrival and checked in to a motel in Darwin as the sun went down. This truly was like a holiday. They had been assigned six rooms in a secure part of what looked to them like a lovely hotel. Abebi and Yetunde looked on wide-eyed as they walked into their room. It even had a balcony and a big bed for Mum and Dad. There was a TV up on the wall and a little cupboard with a kettle, tea and coffee, and biscuits. Charles opened a packet of biscuits and offered one to his girls who were clearly astonished that he had brazenly ripped open the packet with a smile. This was living! A knock at the door signalled a meal arriving and Charles accepted two trays of hot food and cold drinks. Abebi was shocked at how nicely they were being treated.

He worked out the TV and it flickered to life, and the ABC TV news was playing. Charles was transfixed. He hadn't watched TV in months. There was news of empty and decaying immigration detention centres, pictures of boats being intercepted by police. Western Australia, Port Hedland, Christmas Island and Woomera were all mentioned, places that Charles had heard about previously. He knew that they could end up at one of these places, or even back in Papua New Guinea at an immigration processing centre. He was worried, but it was not going to stop him enjoying the moment. He flicked the remote control and football came on the TV. It was Australia, the Socceroos, playing in a game against what looked like Brazil, but not in their famous yellow shirts. Charles sat down on the end of the bed and the girls joined him. Abebi knew Tim Cahill from watching Premier League back in Zambia, and Charles pointed out David Luiz and Tom Rogic as other players they should watch. It was 1–0 with only a few minutes gone and there was a good crowd in what appeared to be a huge stadium in Australia. Charles was puzzled as to why no one had mentioned it during the day after listening to the radio on the bus and being in the airport. Perhaps football wasn't a big thing in this country.

Adenike had started to work through their belongings and was already filling up the sink in the room, pumping her fist at finding some laundry detergent under the sink to start washing some underwear. Who knew how long they would be staying here, so they had better make themselves at home.

Chapter 9

Adelaide

The community housing agent, Alina, a confident young lady with a cheery smile and the hint of a laugh as she spoke, placed the four separate keys on the kitchen bench. She made sure Charles knew which one was which before picking them up again and threading them onto a red keyring that had her details written inside the clear plastic window. Charles smiled warmly. Adenike was already checking through the kitchen, and the girls were running through the back garden, kicking up dust as they went. Alina offered to give them a lift to the local supermarket, but Charles had taken note of where it was on the way and declined the offer.

Two months had passed since they had been relocated to Darwin. A proposed move to an RAAF base in Western Australia to be processed as refugees fell through when the applications of the current inhabitants from Afghanistan were delayed, and a move to a remote detention centre in South Australia was aborted when the government prevented it from reopening thanks to the protests of the local community. It looked as though they were going to spend an indefinite amount of time in Darwin. Summer had just started, and the humidity was high. Charles and Adenike had enquired about schooling for the girls, but it was deemed too close to the end of the year to start anything new. They would have to wait until the beginning of February to start a new year. Even then it was not guaranteed that they would get a place at a local school, and without a status of refugee, or any status, for that matter, they were in limbo. So when they had an unbelievable 24 hours in the middle of December, it came as a total surprise.

Firstly, thanks to the persistence of Edouard, who was living in the room next door, the group were processed as refugees; a group of officials came to the motel and went from room to room to verify all their details, and they were told they were being granted asylum in Australia. A second pair of officials, this time in suits, despite the hot and sticky conditions, took each family through their individual circumstances and what they were to expect from now on. They would all be housed in the community, although this might not be in Darwin—it could be anywhere in the country—and they could apply for benefits and look for employment as part of their Temporary Protection Visas. The group of 20 had already been reduced to 16 when one of the families was deported back to Sudan; Charles had discussed the father's past and his long list of felonies and had suggested that it might be difficult but was still gutted to see them leave in tears.

The group had formed the dynamics of a large family. The three soldiers were the lovable rogues; the three families had their children all mix together. Edouard and his wife, Marie, hailing from the troubled Central African Republic, were both teachers and started to give the children some semblance of schooling. Aicha and her sister Zara were the life of the party, always happy to chat, play games and entertain the children.

This sudden good fortune of being granted asylum, most likely due to the lack of options to process the group, meant that they would probably all be split up. And that was exactly what happened. First the three teenage soldiers were sent to Sydney, then another family was relocated to Cairns in North Queensland. Charles and his family watched on as the rest of the group disappeared within two days, Aicha and Zara to outback South Australia and Edouard and his young family to Sydney too. That left Charles, Adenike, Abebi and Yetunde all alone at the motel for one night. It was the evening of a ferocious thunderstorm, but the peaceful night that followed the light display would be their last in Darwin. The next morning they were picked up by a minibus and accompanied onto a commercial flight to Adelaide. The chaperones stayed with them until they arrived in Elizabeth Park, where they were joined by the bubbly Alina at an address deep in the northern suburbs.

The moment Adenike walked through the front door of the small multi-coloured brick house, she gasped audibly. Abebi didn't know if it was in surprise, horror or delight, but she walked in with her hand over her mouth as if trying to hold back her words. Alina walked ahead of them and dropped her zip-up document holder by the kitchen sink. She walked over to the back window and opened the blind, the sun lighting up the whole living space. The girls stared around themselves in wonder. Adenike chuckled to herself.

"This is a new house!" said Charles with the hint of a question in his voice.

"Oh, it's not new," said Alina. "Maybe 20 years old. But it has been refurbished in that time and the last tenants were lovely people."

The house may not have been new, but it was certainly pristine. There was a laundry area between the kitchen and the back door, a big open living area with a large wooden table and chairs. Alina showed Charles and Adenike through the hallway to the bedrooms. There were two large bedrooms and a small study, and the final room was a bathroom. There were beds for everyone, built-in cupboards and plenty of storage space. Adenike looked at Charles as though they had hit the jackpot.

"And this is ours?" asked Charles, happy to keep the conversation going. "How long can we stay here?"

"You have this for the duration of your visa and potentially beyond," she said. "Depending on how things go from here. I understand you are planning to stay in Australia?"

They both nodded. The girls were squealing with delight outside and laughing.

Alina opened some more blinds, and they could see the back garden, the plumes of dust rising with each footstep the girls took. They had found a barely inflated football and they were already setting up goalposts from the bits and pieces scattered around the garden. It was a joyous scene; Abebi directing, Yetunde fetching, and they had two goals marked out in quick time. With the keys safely back on the keyring and in Charles' hand, Alina left them with another cheery smile, popping her head out the back and waving to the girls who waved back with broad smiles on their faces. The Ngoms were home.

Chapter 10

Cobblers

Abebi and Yetunde were inseparable. The family had spent almost half a year planning and making the journey from Africa, through Indonesia and Papua New Guinea and finally to Australia. The only contacts the family had were fellow arrivals from the boat who could be anywhere in the country by now. They had no mobile phones, no computer, very few belongings, but they had just scored a palace to live in, in what looked to be a fabulous area of a big city.

It was hot, a similar heat to where they had originally started their fantastic journey, and there were more flies than Charles could remember. And the mosquitos, they were something else! The practicalities of living in the suburbs became evident when Charles ventured to the supermarket in the late afternoon, retracing the route they had driven in the minibus. It was only a five-minute walk. He had made a list of things to buy, and had a handful of single-use EFTPOS cards that had been provided when they arrived in Adelaide. A council clean-up had been happening in the street, and there was all manner of furniture, the pre-Christmas clear-out allowing everyone to stock up with new items in the Boxing Day sales. Charles was still picking up items—lamps, bedside tables, a dartboard, paintings and old books—and dropping them back in the front garden of his new house an hour later, still not having made it to the shops.

Charles arrived back home to find the girls in the bath having a real scrub. Mum was combing Yetunde's hair and it was proving to be quite a performance. They had found the linen cupboard and had used nearly all the towels already and bubbles were everywhere. The beds were all made and there was already a load of washing clunking around in the ancient-looking top-loader. Charles felt like the king of the castle and went poking around in the shed outside. There was a manual lawnmower, although there was so little grass, he would only need it for the front. There were all manner of light globes, cleaning products, barbecue utensils, paint tins, rollers and brushes, and a few rudimentary tools.

Night was falling and they had found the light switches. Charles cooked up some *nshima*, a simple dish that he often made to make them feel at home, after finding the right ingredient in the flour aisle in the supermarket, and made a stew of vegetables and broth. They sat down at their big wooden dining table, covered in marks, stains and scratches, and ate their first home-cooked meal in their new home. Charles even had a chocolate treat for the girls, which they shared with their parents. They were clean. They were safe. Charles and Adenike held hands across the table as the girls sang to each other; it was a perfect family evening.

The family set about making a home in Adelaide, and to them, it was so exciting. They had just enough money to live on, and Charles even opened a bank account for them, depositing the remaining US dollars from his now flimsy envelope, which at least gave them a start at savings. He signed up for a mobile phone and made contact with some of their fellow refugees from the boat journey. Charles and Adenike were allowed to work, albeit for only three months at a time, so Charles took the time to research the shoe stores, cobblers and even a shoe manufacturer, putting together a resume at the local library and taking it around to every one of the businesses. He would leave early in the morning on the bus and had covered the whole of Adelaide's footwear industry in two weeks.

Back at the house, Adenike and the girls were making their home beautiful. A stack of home magazines from the street garbage had given them all sorts of ideas, and they set about painting some furniture and making a big go at renovating the back garden. A roster on the fridge had all their tasks, and watering the back garden was a big one, doing so several times a day when it wasn't raining to make sure the grass took hold, and the vegetables they planted grew. The local neighbourhood was friendly enough; they met their close neighbours out in the front garden and whilst they could sense hesitancy from them, they could be relied upon to help. Adenike even mowed the elderly neighbours' front lawn and got some old clothes for the kids in return.

Charles bounded through the door one day and planted a kiss on Adenike's lips. He was flustered and home early.

"I got the job!" he cried.

"Wow, where?" asked Adenike excitedly.

"It's only just down the road," he said excitedly. "I walked in and handed my resume to the man at the desk. We got talking, and he had just lost his last employee. He showed me around and asked me a lot of questions. He then let me mend a pair of boots, it was so good."

Charles was almost babbling.

"And he then asked when I could start, and I said today, right away," he continued. "So, I did three hours of work with him, and he showed me where everything was. It was so good. He gave me some laces and some potatoes at the end and told me to come back tomorrow."

Adenike cuddled her husband and the girls looked on with beaming smiles.

"It's the lucky country, I tell you," she said.

Chapter 11

Baby

"Oh my god, how black is your skin?" asked one girl, trying not to sound snide or nasty.

"Your lips are amazing," said another.

"Can I feel your hair?" came the next.

This had been an almost daily occurrence at Abebi's new high school. She didn't really know how to take it. On one hand, she enjoyed the attention; on the other hand, she knew that there were some casual racists amongst the cohort, and there was even some jealousy.

Abebi's family had settled well into life in the northern suburbs of Adelaide; her father Charles had been working five days a week at the leather sales and repair store, part shop and part workshop, and was possibly the happiest Abebi had ever seen him. The family home was looking amazing, the backyard a lush green after months of careful tending by Adenike; they had fenced off an area to keep chickens, which was a focal point for the local kids, who would come and help find the eggs in the morning. The inside of the house looked like a Spanish villa, all freshly painted in white and homemade shutters on the outside of the windows. Those magazines had come in handy. Yetunde was still at the local primary school and had made a small group of friends; she was quite precocious and had quickly adapted to her new life as if it were completely normal. Abebi, on the other hand, had taken time to adapt to school life, and her final year at primary school, when she outgrew the traditionally tall girls, was a little shaky.

Abebi's newfound height, which was most obvious in the final term of primary school after the October holidays, brought even more attention on her. Luckily, she had the support of the kind physical education teacher who recognised that she was struggling with her newfound stature. The twice-weekly 'posture session' that Miss Matata ran for Abebi and two of the taller boys was priceless in keeping Abebi from hunching over and trying to make herself look the same height as everyone else. By the time primary school was over and she had made a striking mark on the end-of-year photos, she was looking very much like a young woman.

Primary school sport was fun. Abebi was exposed to sports that she had never tried before and she really enjoyed basketball and AFL, even though she still couldn't get the rules by the end of the year. Football, though, or soccer, as everyone seemed to call it, was her one true passion. Even though there was no school team, they had a football carnival which had one all-girl team competing against the younger boys. Abebi showed a lot of skill and determination and she was always the player who would be getting her body in the way or reaching with her long legs to frustrate the boys. She earned a lot of respect from the boys and from the watching mass of students.

Abebi had been at high school for two weeks when the fields had dried up enough for morning break and lunchtime to move outdoors and away from the concrete playground. The less self-conscious children were playing games, running around without a care in the world. A group of boys from Year 7 had started up a small-sided football game alongside a field of older boys who were taking it very seriously. The younger boys had five on six, and Abebi moved closer to see if the five players were coping. They weren't. Lunchtime was only halfway through. Abebi procrastinated for a minute and then raced to fetch the ball after the six-player team had scored another goal.

"Hey, would you like to play?" asked one of the players.

"I'd love to," said Abebi without hesitation, looking towards where the voice had come from.

"You're on our side," came the voice.

Abebi looked at the young face with pretty eyes and realised that it wasn't a boy at all.

"Ah, wow," said Abebi, feeling stupid as she dropped the ball at her feet and played it to her new teammate. "I didn't even notice …"

"Don't worry," said the girl. "I'm Josie. You're Baby, right?"

Abebi smiled.

"It's Abebi," she said, "but I guess it does sound like Baby!"

"All right, numbers are even," she said, turning to her dominant opponents. "We're back in the game."

Josie was a terrier. She pushed and pulled her opponents and wouldn't give them a moment on the ball. Abebi hadn't seen anything like it. With the sides now level in personnel, she could show what she was made of. Their team pulled a goal back within a minute after Josie played a cross-field ball right onto the head of her teammate, who glanced the ball goalwards. The bag acting as the far post was perfectly angled to deflect the ball in without any doubt of it being a goal, and the players all rushed in to congratulate the scorer.

The first bell sounded, and the players took that as the final whistle. There was no injury time or playing to the last goal. The rules were obviously set by the older kids who had passed them down through generations. Abebi walked into class looking dishevelled and beaming with sweat. Two of her teammates and one of the boys from the opposition were in her class, too, and they all radiated, red-faced and beaded with perspiration.

Josie caught up with Abebi at the end of school.

"Hey, Baby, you can really play," she said.

"You're the one who can play," said Abebi. "Those boys didn't know how to handle you."

"They think they're so good," she said with a scowl, "but I knew it was just because they had more players. That Stuart, he never wants to play on my side. We always play short."

"Well, I'd love to play tomorrow," said Abebi.

"Cool," said Josie. "We'll show them who's boss, eh?"

Josie walked off in the opposite direction with a smile; Abebi was setting off for the 45-minute walk home. They were both delighted.

Chapter 12

Inter

Abebi was so keen to tell her dad all about her playing football, and was disappointed when he wasn't at home yet. She gave her mum a big hug when she walked in and sat for a moment as Yetunde did some homework, watching how she would make everything so neat. There was a sound of gravel churning out the front of the house, a car pulling up. Adenike glanced out of the window, and then did a double-take, her eyes widening and a look of delight on her face. Abebi and Yetunde didn't know what was going on, and bounded after their mum to the door.

There was Charles, standing proudly in front of a battered old car with different-coloured panels and rust along the bottom of the doors. He had his arms crossed as if posing for a photo.

"Is this ours?" asked Adenike.

"What do you think, kids?" asked Charles. They both made for the rear doors, choosing the sides that they had chosen the last time they owned a car back in Zambia.

Charles and Adenike stood and watched the girls scramble into the back seat and click in their seatbelts as if they were off for a picnic. Charles got in and started it. The engine hummed and he turned up the music on the radio to full blast, so much so that the girls were screaming and laughing with their hands over their ears. The Ngoms had wheels. This would change everything.

The car changed very little actually in the first two weeks. It sat in the driveway and got a thorough clean, Adenike scrubbing the interior and polishing everything that could be polished, and it seemed like they would never take it out. When Charles offered to drop the girls at school one Friday, they were filled with excitement. After dropping Yetunde at her primary school, even parking up and walking in with her to greet the teachers, they arrived at Abebi's school. Abebi stepped out of the car in front of a group of boys and all the heads turned. Charles looked on, amazed. Abebi waved goodbye to her dad and she could see his broad smile through the windscreen. This was a proud moment for Charles in more ways than one.

Abebi started to really enjoy school. She felt comfortable in classes and surprised herself how confident she was about asking for help when she didn't grasp a concept. But the recess and lunch football games were the highlight. She would always be on Josie's team, and they would conjure up some fabulous moves and intricate plays, the one-two used liberally to dramatic effect. At lunch at the end of the week, as the first bell sent them scarpering to find their bags and race back to class, Josie stopped Abebi and put her hand on her arm.

"Baby," she said slowly, "I have trials on Sunday for Salisbury Inter."

Abebi had no idea what that was. It was a sentence with no context or meaning to her.

"You should come along and see if you can get in the team," continued Josie. "You're so good."

Abebi didn't know anything about the football system in Australia. She had heard the boys talking about playing trial games on the weekend and moaning when the rain had washed out two weekends at the start of term. But she had no idea that girls played football and was compelled to ask Josie about it.

"Where is Salisbury Inter?" she asked, before pondering. Dad had a car. It didn't matter where it was. "What happens at trials?"

Josie looked stunned. As if someone as clearly talented as Abebi wouldn't know what trials were.

"Trials, you know," she said.

Abebi looked at her blankly, hoping for more.

"When you go along with 50 other girls and play loads of football, and they choose squads of 15, and you sign up and you get a shirt and you play every weekend in a competition. You know?"

"Ah, that sounds great," said Abebi. "Where is it and when? Do I just show up? Do I need to put my name down?"

"Just leave that with me and I'll make sure your name's down and they're expecting you," said Josie. The second bell sounded and they started running. "It's Sunday afternoon at 5 p.m. I'll see you at the end of school."

Sure enough, Josie was waiting for Abebi at the end of school. They continued their conversation from earlier on.

"So, the trials are on at 5 p.m. Be there at about 4.30 p.m. I like to get there early and we can have a kick before. It's at Underdown Park. You know it?" asked Josie.

"Can you write it down for me?" asked Abebi. She grabbed the piece of paper she kept in her shirt pocket to record any important information. Josie looked at her with a puzzled expression, then took the paper and wrote down the name of the park and the road it was on.

"There," said Josie. "So I'll see you tomorrow, right, Baby?"

"Ha ha, you don't think I'll be able to find it, do you?" laughed Abebi.

"If you're not there, I'll come looking for you," said Josie and she walked off with a skip.

"Oh my god, Dad!" said Abebi, the street directory on her lap.

Charles was sweating. It was 4 p.m. and they had no idea where they were going, but Abebi's dad was a picture of calm.

"We're not far away, I can sense it," he said with a hint of a chuckle in his voice.

This had been the first time they'd been in this part of town, and they had passed a park with trees where you couldn't see through, but the names of the streets didn't match the names of the streets in the street directory.

"Can you ask someone?" asked Abebi.

"Ha ha, I don't need to ask anyone," said Charles. "Here, give that book to me; I'll work it out."

Abebi was stressing. She wanted to be there with time to spare. She already had her football gear on, her prized Bolton Wanderers shirt and the boots that her dad had found in a box at work and lovingly restored. They were getting their first workout today. Charles pulled over and picked up the street directory, Abebi taking a moment to let go of it. He looked at it and followed the route that they took from home with his finger and then sat back slightly when he realised where he had gone wrong. He ran his finger along some roads in the directory and kept looking at it while placing it back in Abebi's lap. She looked at him with the look that only a tween daughter can give their father, and he caught her eye and smiled.

"Only a few minutes away, my darling," he said, and quickly flicked the car into first gear and pulled away slowly, whistling a nondescript tune as he did.

Chapter 13

Reds

They arrived at 4.20 p.m. There were already people there and the carpark was busy. The younger teams were finishing up their trials, but they found a spot and Abebi jumped excitedly out of the car when she spotted Josie. Charles was left wondering what the rush was, and saw his daughter sprinting over to a friend and grabbing her shoulders from behind. He looked on as she checked out her friend's shirt and was then introduced to what looked like her parents and watched as they looked at ease with each other. This was exactly what Charles had hoped for. He got out of the car and walked over. Abebi saw him and introduced her dad proudly to her friend and to her friend's mum and dad, getting their names right first time too.

Charles shook both of their hands and his beaming smile was infectious. The girls ran over to where another group of youngsters were congregating and Charles could see that Abebi was making new connections straight away.

"I'm so happy that your daughter invited Abebi today," said Charles.

"We're excited to have her here," said Josie's dad. "Josie said she was a gun player. She'll have a great chance of getting into the top team."

"Oh, let's not get carried away," said Charles. "Let's just see how she fits in with the other girls first."

"Where are you from, Charles?" asked Josie's dad. His name was Matthew.

"We're from Elizabeth Park," he replied, before cottoning on to what he meant. "Via Zambia."

"Oh, wow," said Matthew. "I spent some time in Dar Es Salaam for work back in the day. I think I went to Zambia to see some waterfalls. Beautiful country."

"Ah yes," said Charles with a pause. "But it is a country with many troubles, especially for an immigrant from Senegal."

"You love your football, don't you?" asked Matthew rhetorically. "Let me guess, you're a Manchester United fan."

"Ha ha, guilty!" said Charles. "I live as close to Manchester as the average Manchester United fan. One day I'll make it to Old Trafford. And you?"

"Oh, I don't have a team as such in the Premier League," said Matthew. "I like the local game though. I have my Adelaide United membership; we all do."

Matthew pulled up his jacket to reveal the red shirt of the hometown club.

"We're heading there tonight and I have a spare ticket," he continued. "Would you be okay if Abebi came along with us tonight?"

"Wow, that is so generous," said Charles. "I know what the answer will be if I ask Abebi. I'll say yes, although I don't know what she'll wear."

"Don't worry about that," said Matthew. "We've got plenty of spare shirts."

Charles walked over to Abebi and asked her if she would like to go with Josie's family to the A-League game after the trials. Abebi's eyes widened and she looked at Josie and her new acquaintances and looked as if she were going to burst. She hugged Charles with all her might.

"This is the best day of my life!" she whispered in his ear.

The trials ran like clockwork. Most of the girls knew exactly what to do. The confident man who was running the day walked to the gate that separated the field from the carpark and called out for trials for Under 12s and 13s. All the girls in the carpark swarmed through the small gate and they started kicking balls around with the other coaches who had just finished the younger age group.

Charles took a position next to Matthew, perched against the fence. Matthew zipped open a cool bag and offered Charles a beer. It seemed like the most Australian thing to do and Charles gladly accepted the gift. It was in a dark bottle with a green label and the contents seemed cloudy when he held it up to the light; the first mouthful made his lips purse. He clinked bottles with Matthew and with another lady, and the conversation flowed as Abebi went through the process on the other side of the fence.

Abebi was full of enthusiasm, but she was hesitant when put on the spot, as if she didn't understand the instructions from the coaches. She tried not to be at the front of the line for new exercises, so she could see what they were meant to do. The terminology was alien to her, and when the coach yelled out "weaker foot" she didn't understand. Once they were split into groups for a game situation, that's where Abebi came to life. The six-a-side game on a small field was just how she had played previously in the park with her friends, and was just like at school with the boys. Abebi was up against Josie.

Abebi's height made her a little ungainly, but her close skills and long legs that could reach around players to win the ball gave her a massive advantage over the much smaller girls of her age. She played a through-ball at one stage that her teammate didn't read, and she adapted her game after that, making sure the passes were firm and to the feet. She moved around the field quickly and was involved in everything good that her team did. The inevitable head-to-head with

Josie saw Abebi defending and Josie breaking clear. Not only did she catch her, but she slid in and won the ball, sending Josie clattering to the ground.

"I'm so sorry, so sorry," she said, grabbing Josie to see if she was okay.

Josie rolled over slowly and then sprang to her feet, chasing after the next ball, leaving Abebi stranded. In the next break in play, while the coaches sorted out changes to the sides, they shared a laugh.

When the final whistle sounded, it was long and loud, the coaches clearly ready for a break after a long afternoon. The girls were told that the full squads for the season would be announced by email during the week and that training would start the week after. The end was so abrupt that Abebi simply stood with her hands out, looking around, as if she'd missed something.

"Come on, Baby," shouted Josie, and she snapped out of her trance and raced after her friend.

Chapter 14

Hindmarsh

Abebi and Josie stood at the top of the steps and looked down on the magnificent Hindmarsh Stadium playing surface below. What a sight! They were sitting in the main stand and the game had already kicked off; the trials had only left them 20 minutes to get there and even with Matthew's efficient driving, they couldn't make the 6.30 p.m. start. Still, the lack of people outside the stadium made getting in quite easy.

Josie was decked out in Adelaide United kit, tracksuit pants and red home shirt, with a United scarf too. Abebi had a borrowed shirt, a little small on her and a little faded, but it was obvious who she was barracking for.

"Look, there's Diego Castro!" shouted Josie excitedly.

Sure enough, the Spanish star was patrolling the centre of the field, and the noise levels rose when he received the ball.

"You do know Diego Castro, right?" asked Josie with a laugh.

"Oh yeah, he plays for Perth Glory," was all Abebi could say. Adelaide were up against the Glory; it said so on the scoreboard, and it was obvious. The small pocket of away fans was singing it right at that point, too.

"Well, durrr!" said Josie, smiling.

They took their seats once they realised they were blocking the view of those around them, making sure they took a longer route to avoid disturbing the fans already seated. Abebi was almost speechless. The sight of the stadium from the outside was one thing;

going through the turnstiles was a bizarre and unexpected thrill, and seeing the pristine field for the first time was amazing. Matthew filled in Abebi with the context of the game. Adelaide were enjoying a great season by their standards, but Perth Glory were looking very much like favourites to take out the A-League premiership. It was clear who needed the points the most and which team was favourite. Josie had switched off and wasn't listening while Abebi lapped up the extra information that would make the game that much more enjoyable.

The way the crowd reacted to the flow of the game fascinated Abebi. The fans were very loud and not afraid to shout out when something didn't go their team's way. Adelaide looked as good as their opponents for most of the first half that was action-packed, but there was uproar when Perth Glory broke en masse and a scrappy shot was deflected into the goal, Diego Castro being announced as the scorer. Abebi watched as the purple shirts of the away fans bounced while all around her were groans and tuts. She looked at the people around her, mostly resigned looks on their faces as if this were a common occurrence. As the referee started looking at his watch, Josie got up and signalled to Abebi to follow her. They ran down the steps as quickly as they could and to the side of the tunnel just as the half-time whistle sounded.

It was all action; people poured out of the tunnel just before the players poured in, the half-time entertainment started, mini football games and the Fox Sports reporters' interviews were underway. The ball crew went past and Josie held out her hand and got high-fives from the young girls and boys. Abebi looked on in admiration.

"You know the ball boys?" she said, shocked.

"I'm one of them," she said, smiling. "I couldn't be here on time today, so I missed out, but I'm usually in the group."

"Wow, that's amazing!" cried Abebi. She thought it was the coolest thing on the planet. Her friend Josie was some kind of superstar.

"Hey, we'll see if you can do a game one day?" asked Josie.

"Oh, wow," said Abebi. "You could do that?"

"We can always ask!" replied Josie with a smile.

The two girls walked around the stadium. They were joined by two other young girls doing the same thing. This was thrilling to Abebi. She had never seen so many people at a football game, and Josie just seemed to be so relaxed, walking around without a care in the world. Abebi thought of how protective her dad was to her, about how strict he would be to make sure she was home on time from school and to trust no one. Here, she could walk freely and do whatever she wanted.

The arrival of the players back onto the field prompted the two of them to race up the stairs back to their vantage point to take in the second half. The half was maybe 15 minutes in, and Adelaide had looked the most likely to score next. Craig Goodwin crossed time after time, and it looked as though they would eventually break through and equalise. At one point, everyone was standing in anticipation as a shot flew just over; Josie was jumping up and down in despair, and even her dad had his head in his hands. The game was poised. This was exciting.

Heads were back in hands with 20 minutes to go though as a long ball was controlled perfectly by the heavily tattooed Perth striker who strode on to strike a low shot past the keeper for a lovely goal. That would surely kill the game, but no, it prompted a frantic finish. Adelaide did everything they could to get back into the game, but they couldn't find that elusive goal. The final whistle was met with boos. Abebi couldn't believe it. She had been utterly enthralled. She was clapping as the players approached the tunnel, and was so happy to see the players applaud back. She was convinced they were clapping at her and she gave a wave.

To say that Abebi was swept away by her evening at Hindmarsh Stadium would be an understatement. The girls had run back down to the tunnel area and found a spot to lean against the fence. The players filed past, not too dejected. Josie got another scribble on the back of her shirt to go with the other ineligible signatures, and instructed the player, a South American-looking guy, to sign the front of Abebi's, which he did with a big smile as she stretched out the front of the shirt to make it easier.

In the car back home, she couldn't understand how little they talked about the game. Abebi wanted to go through everything that she had seen today, but the conversation seemed to go every other way and she felt frustrated. Once she had been dropped at her door and Charles came out to shake Matthew's hand and thank him, she couldn't stop talking. She told her mum everything, from the moment they arrived at the stadium to the moment they left, only stopping for a short while when Yetunde had finished with the bath. She picked up the conversation as soon as she got out of the bathroom and asked her mum to come into her room so she could keep telling her about it.

She saved all the talk about the trials for her dad. Charles was keen to give her feedback and made sure she knew what she did well and what she could improve on, but again, it was Abebi who did all the talking. She was wired. Even when the light was turned off, and the girls should have been settling down to sleep, Yetunde wanted to know more about her sister's adventures. Abebi finally realised that Yetunde had dropped off to sleep, and she closed her eyes, vivid memories of the day still rolling around her mind. Abebi was hooked. This was something she wanted more of.

Chapter 15

Hook

Life in Adelaide was good; at least, it was good through Abebi's eyes. They had all been warned that they would encounter racism, however casual or even unintentional, and Abebi had learned to ignore the stares and keep a bright smile on her face wherever she went. Her mum had integrated into local life, finding a group of mums from Yetunde's school who were happy to have each other around for coffee after school drop-off. A chance conversation with one of the young mothers led her to be interviewed for a cleaning job at a local hardware store. It was one of those stores that had everything under one roof, and there was a cafe and toilets that needed to be cleaned at the end of the day. Charles wasn't too happy that his wife would be going out late at night and felt that she would be better off at home making the family run better. Adenike, though, had decided that she wanted to bring in some money to help make their lives a little easier.

It was at her new workplace that she encountered a very unpleasant man who took pleasure in calling her names and making derogatory remarks about what she was wearing and how she spoke. She felt powerless and tried her best to ignore him, but he persisted, thinking that he was being funny. He was always rostered on at the end of the day, and she would dread coming in after the lovely walk there to be told that she was dressed like a clown; her head tie, or *gele,* as she called it, was beautiful and all the mums at school remarked on her array of coloured materials that she cycled through each week. But to this man, it was too different. He would stand and smirk as she worked away, throwing out barbs for no reason at all.

"Hey, Ad-Nicki, you've missed a bit," he would helpfully offer.

"Hey, Mrs Black, you're not very good at this, are you?" was another.

"Wow, if I turn off the lights, I can't see you," was one to make her clench her teeth and smile as he flicked the lights on and off.

Adenike was quite a powerful lady with big shoulders and taller than her oppressor, but she had the patience of a saint and a bubbly outlook that made most people smile. It all got to her one night, and Abebi found her sobbing at the dining table. A cuddle from her daughter was enough to brighten the mood and it all ended in smiles, but she told Abebi what the man had been saying.

"Mum, I get that at school sometimes," said Abebi. "I just smile, sometimes shake my head and look confused, and just continue doing what I'm doing."

That was enough for her mum to stand up and pick up her daughter in a bear hug.

"Who's my little girl who's growing up to be a fine woman?" she said. Abebi smiled and hugged her some more.

They had a great relationship, and whenever her mum was at work, Abebi would do all the things that she would do for Yetunde: making an afternoon snack, cleaning up, putting on the washing, and helping with homework. It worked, and when Charles got home, he started the cooking, and the three of them would eat together at the table and share their stories, sometimes joined by Adenike if she caught the early bus.

One evening, she came in quite early, and her smile suggested that they should ask her why she was smiling.

"So, this horrible man at work," she started telling them, "he swore at me, and that was the last straw. So I walked over to him and asked him to repeat what he said to my face."

Abebi and Yetunde were transfixed. Charles had a feeling he knew what was coming.

"I grabbed his phone out of his hand and put it on the counter. I grabbed him under the arms and lifted him onto one of the hooks behind the counter where we hang our bags. I hooked him by the shirt collar. You should have seen him. He was dangling there, thrashing his feet around, going red in the face."

The girls couldn't believe what they were hearing.

"And then I picked up his phone and took a video of him. I asked him if he wanted to repeat what he had just said and he shouted it again. So I flicked through his contacts and found the boss' number and sent through the video."

Charles had his hand across his eyes, peeking through comically.

"You didn't leave him there, did you?" asked Abebi.

"No, no, I just asked him to say my name properly. He couldn't say it at first, but when he was getting even more uncomfortable, he managed to squeak it out and I lifted him off the hook and onto his feet. He didn't say a word. He seemed to have tears in his eyes. I bid him goodnight and left. That's why I'm home a little early."

The girls were smiling broadly. Abebi didn't believe her, but Yetunde had no reason not to; it was a fantastic story. From their mum's expressions and the way she was excited about telling the story, it could well have been true. Charles got out of his seat and hugged her. The girls ran off giggling, still debating whether it was true or not.

Chapter 16

Monkey

Abebi did encounter some problems at school soon after, but took inspiration from her mum's story. At the end of recess one day, one of the girls really let fly when they were lining up to go back inside. Abebi was beaming with sweat.

"URGH, look at her," came a voice from behind in the line just next to her.

Abebi had a feeling it was directed at her, but continued the conversation she was having with the boy in front, who was also red in the face after the quick morning game.

"Stinks like a monkey," came the voice again.

Abebi looked at the boy, Ewen, and they stared at each other with eyebrows raised.

"Looks like she's never washed in her life," was the next cruel barb that cut through the air. Abebi's shoulders flared, and she stood up straight. Ewen had a worried look on his face and almost went to grab her. The lines were a little bit of a rabble while they waited for the teachers. Abebi turned around, and a hush descended on the yard, kids parting to almost make a pathway to the perpetrator to make it easier to recognise who it was. Abebi walked across slowly, looking left and right before standing right in front of her. Her name was Chrissy. Abebi had noticed her staring before but had never said a word to her. Abebi stood almost a head above her.

The crowd seemed to close in, eager to see what was going to happen next. There were no teachers in sight.

"Excuse me?" said Abebi, without a hint of a threat. "Would you like to repeat that?"

There was a pause, long enough to be taken as a 'well then?'

"Looks like she's never washed in her life," Chrissy said slowly, staring madly into Abebi's eyes.

There was another pause. Abebi's blouse was wet with sweat, and beads had formed on her face.

"Might need a scrub then ..." she said, and grabbed Chrissy in a tight hug, making sure that her nose was nestled deep into her underarm. There was a brief struggle, but Abebi held on tight, making sure she rubbed her armpit into her face. The crowd around roared with laughter; it was so unexpected and so defusing.

"What's going on here?" asked a teacher tersely as the crowd dispersed back into their lines, still snickering.

"Chrissy just needed a hug, miss," said Abebi. Chrissy recoiled away, looking flustered, and there was more laughter in her direction as she rejoined her line.

"Back into line, now," said the teacher, who marched to the front and started to dismiss the lines into class. Abebi watched as Chrissy shuffled past her, her hair all frizzed and damp patches all over her blouse.

"That," said Ewen, "was amazing." And their line filed into the doorway and up to their classroom to restart their morning classes.

Chapter 17

Fees

Abebi and Josie formed a majestic partnership that winter season for their club. Josie was a combative midfield dynamo, while Abebi played every position on the left of the field, often roaming up and down the field and using her long strides to good effect. Her crossing left a lot to be desired, and she opted mostly to offload the ball before she got into that situation. Charles thought it was because her legs were so long that she couldn't wrap her foot around the ball quickly enough, but the coaches were sure that she just needed more training and experience. Her tackling, though, was second to none. She had perfected heading, too, often mentioning the name David Wheater, the Bolton Wanderers defender, when she was asked how she became so good at it. That was most often met with blank faces. Bolton were no Chelsea and definitely no Manchester City, the team who had recently taken the English Premier League in dramatic fashion. In fact, Bolton Wanderers had just been relegated from the Championship without a fight, but Abebi wouldn't budge. She was Wanderers through and through, despite only being able to follow them through results in her dad's newspaper every Monday morning.

Inter had their fair share of wins and some defeats, too, but they were never smashed, even against the top teams. With no dedicated goalkeeper, each player would have a turn in goal for half a game at a time in rotation. Sometimes, they had a good player in goal who understood the basics of playing out from the back, but other times, they had a player who simply didn't get it. Abebi would often get frustrated and stand right next to the ball from a goal kick so the goalkeeper didn't stuff up with a stray pass. That tiny pass gave her extra time to sort out her feet and make a big clearance, instead of trying to play out of trouble and inevitably lose possession. It was contrary to the curriculum of the Skills Acquisition Program, but it was effective. Abebi already had a desire to win, and she was aware that trying to play out of defence against some of the stronger teams was utterly pointless.

That individual personality, that adaptability to allow her team to bypass the difficult defensive passing game that was preached through the SAP Program, and the fact that she was more than happy to meet a high ball with a thumping header, made her the standout defender. Whenever the rotation saw her go up front, she was full of running, and the odd half in goal was quite entertaining as she would mix up the passes and learn immediately where not to play the ball from a goal kick.

Josie and Abebi found themselves in front of the headmistress, Ms Turnbull, one day at school. They had arranged a meeting with the head of sports and were very calculated and very formal with their approach. They requested the establishment of a girls' football team to join the local schools' competition for the following year. Ms Turnbull was very impressed. Josie had made a PowerPoint presentation and flicked through the slides on the projector while they took turns putting their thoughts forward. The head teacher and her head of sports played good cop, bad cop very effectively, but even the stone-faced head of sports cracked a smile as they wrapped up their case.

That meeting seemed to have gone nowhere until the final assembly of the school year in the countdown to Christmas. After the formalities and the awards presentations, Ms Turnbull made the announcement that the school would be entering a girls' team into the Adelaide Schools league as a wildcard entry in a new Year 9 girls' competition. There would be no other teams from the school competing and they would be partnering with another school who strangely couldn't field a Year 9 girls' team. It was fate. Josie and Abebi, visibly excited and shocked, were invited to the stage to shake hands with Ms Turnbull, who told the school all about their meeting. A huge round of applause concluded the assembly, and Josie and Abebi were congratulated by their peers from the lunchtime and recess games.

At the same time, the post-season trials were underway for next year's Under 14s women's team at Salisbury Inter. Abebi was asked to come along, even though she had only just finished her Under 12s SAP season. Josie knew a number of the girls in the team and she seemed to fit in; Abebi let her football do the talking and soon she was getting noticed. The four weeks of trials, twice a week, were designed to identify some of the younger talent, those that could make the step up to the full field game.

The girls at the trials were all a year older than Abebi, but she had them all for height and most of them for speed. She wasn't explosive off the mark, but when she got up to full speed, it was impressive. Abebi saw one of the coaches deep in discussion with her dad as they warmed down at the end of the final trial. Charles looked a little agitated and was gesticulating, albeit in a comedic manner, and he ended up shaking the coach's hand and pulling him in for a hug as if to make up for something he said. Abebi was intrigued.

Later that evening, back at home sitting around the big table for a late dinner, Charles sheepishly stared a conversation with his eldest daughter.

"Abebi," he said, shifting uncomfortably before continuing. "I was speaking with the Under 14s coach tonight."

"I know, I saw you."

Charles looked at Abebi.

"They would like you to play with the Under 14s next year," said Charles quietly. Abebi's face beamed.

"I told them that you'll need to wait until you've done your Under 13s SAP," said Charles, recoiling a little just in case. Abebi's face turned immediately to a frown.

"We can't afford to pay the fees just yet," he said with a solemn face. "It's more than double what we are paying now."

Abebi's shoulders had dropped as far as they could possibly drop, but she wasn't going to let the urge to cry take over. The cost of playing football had started to become an issue right around Australia as the Skills Acquisition Program became the gold standard and NPL football was the logical next step. Abebi had heard parents talking about it, and some of the boys at school who played at recess and lunch would often discuss the SAP program and the NPL as the football they'd love to play but can't afford. They were good players too. She was just about to put her elbow on the table and slump her chin into the palm of her hand when Charles spoke again after the longest of silences.

"Just as well the club agreed to pay for half of your fees for next season ..."

Charles hadn't finished his sentence and Abebi was up and catapulting herself at her dad for an almighty hug. She turned and ran to her mum and hugged her too as she sat in her seat and saved the best for her sister Yetunde, who got out of her seat and the two of them jigged along to some imaginary crowd chants as if they had just won the Grand Final. Abebi was going to be playing proper football next year; what a result!

Chapter 18

Port Arthur

The Ngom family were firing on all cylinders. Christmas had been fantastic, and for the first time in Australia, they had taken a holiday. Thanks to a kind lady at one of Adenike's three part-time jobs, she was offered an old shack for three days during the week between Christmas and New Year. It was old but it was immaculately clean and was only a stone's throw from the beach in a small town on the other side of Port Arthur. The weather was simply amazing and they enjoyed three carefree days of sleeping, eating, playing in the sunshine and walking for kilometres on the beach.

Leaving the holiday house meant a quick return to work for Charles and Adenike, but the girls had four more full weeks of holidays before they had to return to school. Charles had his job at the repair shop and also worked a Saturday evening shift assembling market stalls at the Torrens Island fresh food market. That freed up his Sundays that were consistently filled with football. Adenike's typical day saw her open up a fabric store in the local shopping centre at 9 a.m.—the owner was quite old and was becoming less mobile and needed someone to freshen up the store every morning while it was quiet. She would then help with the lunchtime rush at the local RSL, helping with food prep and washing up until 3 p.m. She would have a two-hour break to get the house in order and cook for the evening meal, and then had an office cleaning job down the highway near the girls' school that would see her finish around 8 p.m. It was a long day, but she was surrounded with good people and she was creating quite a network of friends and colleagues.

Chapter 19

Scene

The first Monday of the new year, Adenike decided to take the girls with her to the cleaning job to show them the office and to make them aware of what she did at night-time. Adenike played foreman and had her two labourers running around for her but found that the cleaning part of the job was out of scope for her subordinates. Yetunde dropped a sponge in the toilet and Abebi sprayed way too much product on the sinks in the ladies' bathroom and made a mess that her mum had to quickly rectify. Bringing the girls was starting to seem like a mistake, but they saved time by running around and emptying the waste paper bins and straightening up any furniture that was out of place. They finished half an hour earlier than she would have herself. Yetunde made light work of the vacuuming and Abebi emptied the dishwasher, showing her quirkiness by lining up all the cups, glasses and bowls perfectly in the cupboard. They breezed out of the office building with a spring in their step into a beautiful Adelaide summer's evening.

Adenike was carrying a heavy bag of all the left-over food from an afternoon tea that had been left at the office, and she was beginning to think she should have split the goods into two bags to balance the load. The girls were carrying as much as they could, and they were chatting happily together, every so often involving their mum in the conversation who laughed along with them. They came to the fork in the road where they would cross onto the other side and catch the bus home, and Adenike had already told Yetunde to slow down and be careful as they approached the road in front of the corner pub. A wiry black-haired man and a fierce-looking woman were in their path ahead, scolding a young lady by the edge of the kerb who could have been their daughter. The younger woman was looking very scared and pleading with the couple to leave her alone. The girls stopped and waited for their mum, to fall in behind her for protection. Adenike walked on without breaking stride, but the man lost his grip on the girl and stumbled back and clipped her, falling onto one hand before steadying himself. Adenike stopped, turned square to the man and stared as he stood back up. She was agitated and one of the handles of the bag had snapped.

Abebi and Yetunde had rarely heard their mother get angry, but she started quietly, mumbling something in her native tongue, before finishing her sentence with quite the verbal assault, pointing at the young woman who was in tears on her knees then gesticulating towards the couple. Before she could finish the sentence though, a group of five or six people descended upon Adenike and the girls, one of them stepping in between her and her two children. Yetunde grabbed Abebi's hand and Abebi reached for her mum's. There was a moment of silence as Adenike broadened her shoulders in indignation and at the potential danger, before a tall blond man ran towards the group and, quite unexpectedly, pushed Adenike backwards. She stumbled backwards, letting go of her bags, and fell off the kerb onto her back on the road. There was a look of shock on the faces of Abebi and Yetunde.

The screeching of tyres made everyone look, a passing bus slamming on the brakes, the driver unable to react in time to stop. The driver's face was stunned and he was off his seat trying to apply as much force to the brake pedal as his passengers all rocked forward violently in their seats. Adenike disappeared under the bus and there was a jolt of the wheels before it came to a stop, her lower half sticking out from underneath the bus with her legs crossed in an ungainly manner. There was screaming, gasps and curses from the people on the pavement as the brakes on the bus let out a burst of air. The bus doors opened and the bus driver could be heard apologising to his passengers before quickly bouncing down the steps and racing over to where Adenike was lying.

Yetunde's head was buried into Abebi's armpit, but she was peeking. Abebi stood still, staring at the scene. The crowd around them had dispersed. Two other men went across and gently moved one of Adenike's legs so they were side by side and they both reached under the bus, checking for vital signs. The bus driver was frantic.

"Somebody call an ambulance," he shouted firmly, but he was clearly shocked. "Oh my god, somebody call an ambulance."

One of the men got up off the ground and grabbed the driver's shoulders.

"Can you move the bus away from the kerb a little? I don't want to move her," he said in a reassuring tone that sent the driver back to the driver's seat. The man stood by the open door as another lady warned the oncoming traffic of the manoeuvre that was coming. The driver turned the wheel sharply and reversed until Adenike's face came into the light. She wasn't moving. She looked peaceful, but was clearly limp. The other man was straight to her side, and a distressed-looking lady, dressed up for a night out, appeared holding a defibrillator and had already unwrapped it from its cover. The machine started walking through instructions as she set it down by Adenike's side. There was blood on the road, pooling under her neck as the three got to work heroically to revive her.

Abebi inched closer, Yetunde still clinging to her as tightly as she could. The lady who was directing traffic appeared by their side and put her arm around them both. They could only watch as their mum's clothes were undone and the machine's tentacles attached to her skin. One man was above her, pushing hard against her chest in rapid pulsations, and when he couldn't continue, the other man took over. Sirens could now be heard and, after what seemed like an eternity, flashing lights appeared and two paramedics raced onto the scene, calmly establishing the sequence of events with the two men before taking over and engaging a bigger machine that sent jolts through Adenike's body, but failed to encourage any positive signs.

Abebi and Yetunde hadn't moved. The bags of food had been placed next to them. The lady was still next to them and seemed to be trying to work out what to say. Eventually she got down on her haunches and spoke to the girls.

"My name's Caroline," she said.

She wasn't expecting the girls to offer their names.

"Is there anyone we can call to come and get you?" she asked.

Abebi simply looked over her shoulder towards her mum.

"What's happening to my mum?" asked Yetunde.

There was silence. This was difficult.

"These kind people are looking after your mum," she said with a pause and a flicker of a smile. "They'll take her to hospital."

She struggled to get up and touched Yetunde's hand for balance, who flinched and burrowed further into her sister. She walked the two metres to where the paramedics were still working and had a quick word. She returned to the two girls.

"You can go and hold your mum's hand for a moment," she said, gesturing them to step forward.

The paramedics stopped their pumping and one of them stood up, covered in sweat. The other covered Adenike's chest with her unbuttoned blouse. Abebi and Yetunde both got down on their knees, Yetunde doing as she was told and grasping her mum's hand. Abebi ran her hand through her mum's hair. She looked grey. Her eyes were closed but Abebi could see her eyeballs glinting through her eyelashes. She reached over and felt her cheek softly, the tears welling in her eyes. The young paramedic next to the girls then interrupted and said they needed to get to work. Abebi's instincts kicked in immediately and she gently lifted Yetunde away from her mum and they stepped back to where they had come from and the warm, welcoming face of Caroline.

An ambulance was on scene and the paramedics continued to work as they wheeled the stretcher into the back. Abebi tapped her dad's phone number into Caroline's mobile phone and Caroline took a step back to make the call in semi-private as the paramedics came over to see them. They offered water, taking in plenty of their own fluids after their hard work on their patient's chest. Abebi took a bottle and offered it first to Yetunde, who gulped down the cool water, droplets spilling from the corners of her mouth.

The police were in attendance. The bus driver was sitting on the step of his empty bus, totally distraught. One officer asked if he was okay to take a breath test, and he obliged. His eyes were ringed with red. He looked over at Abebi, with Yetunde still holding tight to her, and caught her eye. He tried to smile and then shuddered, unable to contain his grief, and sunk his head into his hands, crying.

That was the last time Abebi and Yetunde saw their mum. Charles had turned up in the car and taken the girls home. He asked the lady from across the street to be with them while he headed to the hospital, and the girls got ready for bed just like any other day in the middle of school holidays. They didn't speak a word.

Adenike Ngom was pronounced dead on arrival at hospital. The cause of death was officially a heart attack, but she had suffered multiple fractures and internal damage to her organs. Charles knew he would be going to hospital not to be with his wife, but to be confirming her identity, filling out paperwork and saying goodbye.

Chapter 20

Social

The breaking headline in the newspaper the next day was of a race-related hate crime in suburban Adelaide. Footage was released of the incident from the CCTV outside the pub, and it clearly showed a man making a lunge at Adenike, the footage cutting out before she stumbled off the kerb, and it zoomed in on the man's face. It was grainy and dark, and the footage zoomed in and out to show a less-grainy but more distant shot of the man's features.

Charles sat at the dining room table. The two police officers who had been assigned to find out more about yesterday's events turned off the tablet computer and thanked Charles and the girls for their help. Abebi and Yetunde had gone back to their room beforehand in silence and were lying together on Yetunde's bed. Big sister was cradling little sister, just as their mum used to cradle them both, and Abebi was singing the tune that she always used to sing when they were feeling sad.

Two weeks passed, and the perpetrator had been identified and questioned. The flowers in the kitchen were wilted, and Abebi gathered them from the vase and took them out into the garden to throw in the compost bin. She almost stopped herself, thinking about how significant this gesture could be, but she went ahead anyway and returned to clean the vase and return it to the cupboard above the sink.

The girls had a visit from a social worker who had a long chat with them about their mother and left them feeling warm and happy, having shared many memories. Charles was yet to grieve, so it seemed, and the look of disgust written on his face when the police told him that the man who pushed his wife to death had been released from custody due to insufficient evidence was enough to make Abebi retreat to her room in fear. There was support for the family from the neighbours and the local community, with the funeral having been attended by a big crowd, as well as the television crews; this was a story that would not go away. Adelaide, and indeed the whole country, was rocked by the injustice. But nothing would bring Adenike back, and Abebi knew that they would need to adapt quickly to their new life, with the new school year beginning in a few days.

Chapter 21

Boots

"'Tunde," cried Abebi, using her little sister's nickname to suggest that this was a friendly warning. "Come on, we're going to be late."

With their father working longer hours and often up until late at night, Abebi had absorbed the role of mother into her existing role of big sister. The big photo of Adenike by the front door had fingermarks all over it where they all kissed their fingers and touched their mum on the way past. Abebi took the time to wipe it down while she waited for Yetunde to bluster into the living room, almost dressed for school.

"I can't be late," said Abebi, pleading.

Yetunde looked at her blankly and grabbed her packed lunch from the counter and walked over to Abebi, who began to fuss and rearrange. Yetunde offered no resistance. This was exactly how their mum would have fussed over them. The door suddenly opened and in stumbled Charles, carrying a huge black bin liner.

"Ah, my princesses," he said with an air of theatre. "Can I chauffeur you to school today? Special treat for my special ladies."

He struggled on to the dining area and heaved the bag onto the big dining table. The girls looked on, unsure as to what was happening. The urgency to leave had gone, now that they knew they were getting a lift.

Charles picked up the corners of the bag and tipped it upside down; there was a loud tumbling noise as a torrent of football boots, stray shoelaces and dirt cascaded onto the table, some dropping to the floor.

Abebi and Yetunde looked at each other, eyebrows raised.

"Look at this!" said Charles. He was genuinely excited.

"What …? Why have you got so many football boots?" asked Abebi.

"It's the collection from the football boot drive," said Charles. "Remember, they were collecting boots to send to Africa?"

"Right …?" said Abebi, looking at him sideways.

"Well, they've arrived," he said. "Look at them all!"

"Okay …" said Yetunde, totally unimpressed and a little puzzled by the huge pile of dirty football boots.

Charles covered his tracks.

"Well, they were meant for Africa, but when the club found out how much it would cost to send them over, they just sat in the training shed. The coach asked me if I wanted them. I guess they ended up with the Africans after all."

Abebi was already digging through the pile, looking for a decent pair of boots that might be in her size. Charles was picking out the odd shin pad and sock that had found its way into the collection, while Yetunde was half-heartedly picking through the dirty pile, an uninterested look on her face.

Abebi stopped and looked at the clock.

"Dad, we have to go," she said. "Please."

They immediately stopped what they were doing, Yetunde having found a sudden interest in the pile of boots.

"'Tunde," said Abebi firmly. Yetunde let the boot she was holding drop to the table with a clatter. She was playing the part of younger sister and pre-pubescent tween to perfection.

"What are you going to do with the boots?" asked Abebi in the car.

"Ah, well," pondered Charles, "I'm going to find the good ones, repair them the best I can, and sell them."

He was smiling as he drove.

"And the rubbish ones, I'll give to the next football boot drive at some other football club."

Abebi didn't know whether to be impressed at his gall or appalled at his impudence. Yetunde was smiling and nodding. Charles had worked with shoes and boots all his life, and he had the equipment at his disposal to do repairs and make the boots like new, even better. Abebi could see that this was another way of making ends meet and she couldn't help placing her hand over his on the gear stick and they shared a smile.

Chapter 22

Justify

It had been six months since Adenike had gone, and life was settling into a pattern, even if that pattern was totally different to the way things were before. Money had always been tight, but even more so now, and Charles was doing all he could to keep their heads above water. He was a regular at Abebi's youth league games now, and had taken quite an interest in football, always quick to provide a statistic or an anecdote about the beautiful game when they were all together.

Yetunde had been playing her own games too in the younger Skills Acquisition Program, and together with Abebi, their training was taking up every night of the week. Saturday morning was the only time they had to be together at home unless training was cancelled. Abebi had grown even taller and was striking quite a figure when she walked out onto the field, often towering above the unfortunate soul who had to chase her down the wing. There was still a long way to go with her frame though, and she gave the impression of being weak when in fact she was anything but. The focal point of their very existence was the game of football. Abebi knew it, and she feared the day that she would get an injury or was sick and couldn't play. She also feared the day that Yetunde would grow up to be a better player than her, as is often the case with siblings and sport.

Charles had been heavily affected by the loss of his wife and the girls' mother, but he had remained positive and was now becoming quite a jolly man, that guy with the infectious smile. His English was starting to get weathered into an Australian twang, and he was becoming tuned in to the Aussie sense of humour. The hours he spent surrounded by Aussies at the repair workshop, interacting with customers, and at the markets on Saturday night with the crew of workers, were turning him into a local.

Abebi was relieved to have arrived at school a little earlier than usual. Both Abebi and Yetunde were due in the head teacher's office at 8:15 a.m. Abebi knew what this was about; Yetunde would surely know too, but they hadn't talked about it until now.

"Ah, Abebi, Yetunde," said Ms McKenzie with a friendly tone when she walked into the waiting area next to her office. She had obviously just arrived and was carrying a heavy box that made her wobble as though she were about to drop it. "Follow me."

Abebi had already jumped up and was moving in to help her head teacher with the box, but Ms McKenzie strode on, opened her office door and let the box drop with a thump on the floor. She had red marks on her hand where she had been holding the box, and it definitely sounded heavy. Yetunde walked in slowly and the girls both sat down, Ms McKenzie removing the third chair and placing it beside the window.

"I would like to talk about the incident that took place last week," she said, straightening her clothes before sitting down opposite them behind the desk. "Yetunde, can you describe what happened?"

Yetunde looked straight ahead. There was panic in her eyes. Abebi had already been to see Ms McKenzie the day the incident happened and they had agreed to have this meeting. Abebi hadn't talked about it with her sister but had thrown in some suggestive lines to conversations to try and get her to talk.

"Which incident is this?" asked Yetunde after an eternity.

Abebi's eyes widened. If she didn't know which incident this was, perhaps it was one in a catalogue of incidents.

"Mariana Henry," said Ms McKenzie swiftly, without changing her tone.

Yetunde's shoulders curled inwards, and her gaze dropped a little.

"Mariana Henry has bruising all down her arm," continued Ms McKenzie. "We have asked her parents not to involve the police in this matter, but we would like to know what happened to provoke you."

There was a moment of silence.

Abebi shifted in her seat and turned to her sister, awaiting an answer. Yetunde's eyes were moist, her gaze flickered as the tears formed. Perhaps she was reliving the incident in her head.

"'Tunde, please," said Abebi.

Again Yetunde's head bowed further.

"Do you really want to know what Mariana Henry said to me?" said Yetunde, using a clarity of tone that surprised both Abebi and the head teacher. They both jolted back. "Let me tell you." She dug her nails into her palms. "'Your mother jumped in front of a bus to escape from you,'" said Yetunde. "That's what she said to me."

Ms McKenzie rocked back into her chair. Abebi shifted and sat properly on her seat again, nestling her back into the back of the seat. Abebi hadn't known this. What she had known though was that Yetunde had been in an argument with one of Mariana Henry's group of friends earlier in the day, and had accidentally on purpose found herself in the girls' bathroom at the same time as Mariana. According to Ms McKenzie's eyewitnesses, she had gone straight in with a punch, catching her on the edge of the eye, and when the much taller Mariana had retaliated, Yetunde ducked the fist heading her way, moved in with her shoulder and sent her adversary to the floor. According to the other girls in the bathroom at the time, Yetunde had asked, "Is this what it's like to be run over?" before repeatedly stamping on Mariana's arm with her quite solid school shoes. Some of the other girls had then raced in to stop her, while Mariana lay on the floor holding her arm and bleeding from the eye.

"Do you think that justified the action you took?" asked Ms McKenzie.

"No, Miss," said Yetunde sheepishly, but maybe sensing she had the upper hand and wasn't in trouble.

Ms McKenzie thought for a moment.

"I would like you to write a letter of apology to Mariana," she said eventually. "You've never had anything against her before, and I know you worked together in class on a project earlier in the year. Let's start there and let's mend this relationship."

Abebi had crossed her arms, the way that her mum would have done if she was unimpressed with her daughters' behaviour.

"Come and wait outside my office tomorrow morning with the letter, written by hand in your best handwriting, and we will give it to Mariana."

Abebi was sure that this wasn't standard protocol at school, but was relieved that it was such a minor punishment.

"And Yetunde," she continued, looking at Abebi this time. "Lunchtime detention for the rest of the week."

Abebi gave a nod of the head. Still, not a big punishment for a quite premeditated assault on a fellow student.

"Yes, Ms McKenzie," said Yetunde obediently.

That was the last time Yetunde got in trouble at school. It had highlighted that she had some triggers, some boundaries that should not be crossed. She had also given herself a reputation at school as someone who should not be messed with. Abebi had assumed the role of mother, and was assuming the role without any thought of how Yetunde felt. Once they left Ms McKenzie's office and were about to join the hubbub of students rushing through the corridors to go their separate ways to class, Abebi grabbed Yetunde by the arm and hugged her tightly. Yetunde responded by grabbing her big sister around the waist and they stood for a moment as the world moved around them.

Chapter 23

Possibles

There was excitement when the school finally announced that a football team would be happening. They would join the state competition, replacing one of the schools that couldn't field teams in the previous term. It was clear to Abebi that their school was doing this as a favour to the organisers of the competition who had received complaints about too many byes. This was not a football school, and had never entertained the notion of a football team, but the handful of inter-school games that the Year 9 girls had played had been met with nothing but positivity. AFL was the main sport, the first team was revered, and the colours of Adelaide Crows flew proudly on the school flagpoles every Monday morning whenever there was a victory on the weekend. Abebi had not even a glimmer of hope that a girls' team would be forthcoming, but was keen to give the boys' team a go, and there was only one junior team and one senior team.

"Baby, you made it!" said Josie when Abebi turned up at the trial during the final period on a Wednesday afternoon. "I was praying you would be here."

Josie was the star of the Salisbury Inter Under 14s team, and even though results were not fantastic, she was a standout player who bossed the midfield. Abebi had missed the start of the season after her mum had passed away and it had taken a long time for her to work up the courage to return to the training field with her teammates. Her confidence had also taken a knock, and she accepted not being part of the team on the weekend until she had achieved some level of fitness. The five appearances she had made since then were steady, but lacking the bite she had shown the year before that secured her place in the squad in the first place.

"Is it just you and me?" asked Abebi, scouring the group for other girls.

"Of course," said Josie. "We've got to put in a good performance today though. There's only one trial and we have to make ourselves seen. Let's work together, okay?"

Abebi smiled. Girl Power!

"Let's do this!" said Abebi enthusiastically, showing more drive and determination than she had shown for months. This was an opportunity to come up against boys of their own age and they weren't going to take any prisoners.

The group of players was surprisingly big. This would be 25 players down to a squad of 15. Abebi looked around, everyone eagerly listening to the two teachers assigned as coaches for the session. The players were split into two groups, and the more confident of the coaches took the team containing all the boys from Abebi and Josie's lunchtime games, and the rather timid teacher, who didn't seem to know much about the game, took the team containing the girls. It already looked suspiciously like the girls would be in the 'possibles' team, while the all-boys team was the 'probables', albeit based upon a complete guess by the coaches.

Abebi was relieved to be on Josie's team. She was also relieved that they were both starting, and there were only three substitutes, who all looked as if they had never kicked a ball before. In fact, one of the boys was already red in the face and sitting on the ground panting furiously after the single lap warm-up. Abebi's team was given the bibs, the odour coming from the bag hardly inspiring, and it took a couple of turns of the lucky dip to find a bib that looked big enough. There were all sorts of shapes and sizes—some of the boys still fresh-faced and high-pitched, while a few had already been through a growth spurt and were ungainly and awkward. Abebi felt tall, and she was confident with her height. She looked at Josie, who just looked like a footballer even when she was standing still, and they smiled at each other.

The coaches swapped the teams around quite regularly. Abebi had played on the left wing, Josie in the middle of the park, but they both ended up in defence by the time the game was over. Josie had sparkled throughout, beating players with ease, and playing simple passing football, allowing the other players to mess up while she jogged around effortlessly and did everything right. Abebi, on the other hand, was putting in the maximum effort possible and was racing down the line like a gazelle, beating opponents for pace every time she stretched her long legs into a sprint. Her passing too was on point and the coach was roaring at the opposition's wide players to close her down. A long-range left-foot shot from the edge of the area after cutting in saw Abebi smash the ball off the bar with the goalkeeper rooted to the spot. Her tenacity to block a shot on the line soon after earned her hugs from her teammates. This was good football, and both Abebi and Josie knew they were looking good for a spot in the squad.

The self-doubt and expectation of disappointment was enough for Abebi to seek out the coach the next day and ask if she was in the team. All she got was a smile, and was told to "wait until tomorrow" when the squad list would be announced. Josie was also expecting to miss out. It was somehow normal for girls to be excluded from boys' sport simply because they were girls, and she had been the first to go on the attack whenever that arose.

There was a crowd around the sport noticeboard when Abebi arrived the following morning. There was excitement and a lot of chatter. Some boys were high-fiving and there were smiles and laughs. Other faces weren't so jovial. The jostling stopped when Abebi arrived, joined by Josie who had run to catch up with her. Abebi was tall enough to see over the boys' heads, but they parted anyway to let the two girls in. There, at the top of the list, were the names of both of the girls, a 'c' after Josie's name signifying that she was the captain of the team. This was massive. They looked at each other and smiled. The remaining boys roared when they knew that the girls had seen their names in the squad list and it was like a mini dance floor as the boys cheered loudly and jumped around, the girls joining in as well. What a moment. The boys offered clasped handshakes and hugs. It was a peculiar moment, almost like becoming one of the boys, and that wasn't lost on Abebi.

Chapter 24

BBC

Charles had been hard at work at night-time at home repairing football boots. People even came to the door with their favourite pair of boots and he would invite them in and share a glass of the milky wine he always had on hand, some sort of palm wine that a local distiller had given him in exchange for some work. Abebi had tried it and it made her face contort. Yetunde had even tried it and she pretended that she found it okay, but turned down the opportunity to have some more when Charles offered her the rest of the glass. If the boots could be repaired easily, Charles would give them a price and take their telephone number. If the boots were beyond repair, he would let them know, and more often than not the boots would be left behind and Charles could use the material to repair other boots. Abebi had once seen her dad convince someone that their Adidas Predators were unsalvageable, and then saw the glint in his eye once the customer left the house after a few wines, leaving the boots with Charles.

He had quite a range, and they took up a lot of space in the garage. The difference in condition between a typical pair of boots when he got them and when they had been repaired was unbelievable. They were like new boots, and even seemed stiff and smelled like a new pair. The girls were often sent on missions to the recycling bins behind the shopping centre in town, Charles sitting in the car like the getaway driver, as the girls foraged through the cardboard looking for old shoe boxes. He even printed out stickers at work with BBC (Boots by

Charles) and the Nike swoosh underneath that he stuck on the boxes with the size and make of the contents. It was quite the operation, and kept Charles up until the early hours at times.

He made his debut at the markets one Sunday morning, with all football cancelled due to a downpour the day before, and after spending the Saturday night putting up the market stalls and making sure there was one extra, the circle was complete. He had a business. It was cash only. It was cheap too. Brand-new-looking football boots at less than $40 a pair, and plenty of sizes to choose from. He even had a bench for people to sit on and a wooden step with the outline of two feet, with all the sizes written on in black pen. Charles would have a piece of wood that he would place at the toes of the foot on the step and would give advice about sizing depending on the make.

Abebi loved it. Whenever she could, she would help. The Sunday mornings were only ever last-minute affairs if there was no football for the girls, but a three-week run of washouts made him a fixture, and word had got around about his business so much so that he was conspicuous in his absence when the football resumed as the weather cleared. Word of mouth had plenty of people interested, and he would always have a selection of boots in the back of the car for Sunday mornings at Underdown Park or wherever the girls were playing, and it was almost like a car boot sale. Literally.

Abebi stood on the stage at the end-of-year assembly, as proud as she had ever been. The 15 players who made up the junior school team all held a certificate of achievement and their coach had given the most rousing speech to the rest of the school, singling out Abebi and Josie for spearheading the rise of football at the school. The team had started their half-season slowly, coming to grips with the quality of the opposition, but with the incredible leadership of Josie in midfield, they had started to turn narrow defeats into draws until on the final round of the short season, they came up against a school who were looking to qualify for the finals. An incredible display by their goalkeeper, himself an NPL player, and a curling effort from the edge of the area by Abebi were enough to win the game 1–0 with seemingly the whole school watching on. It had been the most thrilling game and even though they had no silverware to show for it, their inaugural season had ended on a high.

The applause rang around the courtyard and the players filed off the stage to be replaced by the towering senior AFL players. The enthusiasm didn't seem as high for their awards. They also hadn't won anything, but had finished high in the placings and it had been considered a successful season. The speech given by their coach was barely motivating. Abebi could feel that the football team had captured the imagination of the whole school and the AFL was considered somewhat as an exclusive sport played by only the biggest boys. It seemed almost elitist.

Abebi and Josie had been retained in the Under 15s by Salisbury Inter. They were now part of the furniture. Christmas came and Charles was delighted when the lady with the holiday house near Port Arthur contacted him and offered the old shack to him for the family. It was such a kind gesture, and one that was offered thanks to the friendship between the lady and Adenike. Charles had no hesitation in accepting, even though the memories might be painful, if only for a short time.

The girls had a great time. Being out of school was fantastic, even having a break from football was refreshing, and they enjoyed their five days in the tiny beachside town. At night, Charles would cook the most amazing meals. He really went to a big effort, having the time to spend doing something he loved. They even had the neighbours over after dinner one night after Charles had bumped into them taking the bin out. Abebi loved seeing her dad like this. She could see that he loved the company, but that he didn't really have the time to relax like this during the rest of the year. She secretly hoped that this annual trip would be a fixture in their lives for many years to come.

Charles was very relaxed with the girls too. He let them stay up as long as they wanted, knowing that Abebi would eventually recognise the signs that Yetunde was reaching her limit and that she would suggestively yawn and stretch to signal that it was bedtime. Yetunde had flipped from being the resenting tween to being the smiley beacon of joy that she always had been. From her bed, Abebi could hear Charles humming to himself as he cleared away the last of the dinner plates, talking to Adenike as if she were there and chuckling to himself. It made Abebi's heart ache and her eyes well up, but it was a lovely feeling and she would drift off to sleep with happy thoughts.

Chapter 25

Throat

Salisbury Inter Girls Youth League Under 15s had the most amazing season that year. They struggled to score goals, but they conceded even less, and slender victories by a single goal to nil, regardless of where the opponent was placed in the league table, would be a feature. Charles and a few of the other dads coined them "boring, boring Arsenal" in reference to the pre-Premier League exploits of the annoyingly successful North London club, but they played very entertaining football despite scoring the majority of their goals from midfield.

The injection of an even younger player midway through the season, stepping up from the Under 14s, changed the equation and they started to convert the chances and ripped some of their adversaries to shreds with their penetrating wing play. Abebi was a big part of that, playing the wing-back role or sometimes pushed up as an out-and-out winger. Where she had seen a dangerous ball in flash straight across the face of the goal earlier in the season, since the introduction of Maya Johnson those crosses were more often than not converted into goals, the predatory instincts of the fresh young striker complementing the fabulous approach play of the team. The season extended well into September following the heavy rain earlier in the year, and the presence of well-groomed people in branded polo shirts of Adelaide United started to get tongues wagging.

Maya was the first to be introduced to the tall lady and the shorter fit-looking man with the intense look in his eyes, when she had scored a late winner in a 2–1 win at Para Hills. The rest of the team were glancing over as their coach Ivan ran them through the good and bad points of the game, and when Maya came jogging over, they all stopped listening and turned their attention to their striking sensation. She ignored the questions and grabbed Abebi and told her they wanted to have a word to her too. Right now. Coach Ivan was by now standing with his arms crossed, incredulously watching as his team chatted amongst themselves. Abebi raised her eyebrows at him and pointed over to where she had been instructed to go and he nodded with a smile. She raced across the field to the VIPs.

"You wanted to see me?" she asked, full of endorphins from the game and peaking in excitement.

"Yes, Abebi, isn't it?" asked the lady. "I'm Suzie, and this is Ryan. We're from Adelaide United. I guess you knew that from our shirts though …"

Suzie held out her hand and Abebi shook it. Ryan didn't offer a shake but his intense stare softened for a moment when he caught her eye. Suzie would do all the talking.

"Now, your surname, N-G-O-M. How do I say that?" she asked.

Abebi smiled. This was something that she was rarely asked, and she rarely corrected anyone who got it wrong.

"The N and the G make an 'nnnng' sound, like 'cominnnng'," said Abebi. "And then just add the '-om' to the end. Innings. The 'g' gets lost in your throat. Try it!"

The confidence that she had just shown surprised herself, but she had rarely been asked the question and she had thought this scenario through in her head for a long time.

Ryan said it, and nailed it first time. Abebi looked at him and nodded her head.

"I'll note that down. Let's see if we get that right next time. Now, the reason we've called you over for a chat is that we would like to invite you to a training session on Tuesday night at our training centre at Playford. Do you know it?"

"Ha, yes I do, it's just around the corner from my house!" said Abebi. "What time do I have to be there and what do I bring? Oh, and what is the training for?"

"This is a training session for Under 15s and Under 16s in the area," said Suzie. "We are approaching the start of the W-League season and we would like to see if there are any youth players capable of stepping into our squad …"

"For the W-League?" interrupted Abebi, as if she wasn't following. "Like, Matilda McNamara and Fiona Worts?"

"Yes, exactly," said Suzie, who seemed to be impressed at Abebi's knowledge of at least two of the names in the Adelaide United women's team.

"Wow!" exclaimed Abebi, putting her hand over her mouth and almost buckling at the knees. She was now talking through a smile that wouldn't go away. "That's amazing. Yes, I'll be there. When is it again? Did you tell me that already?"

Ryan was laughing now.

"6 p.m. start, so be there 15 minutes beforehand and ask for Suzie if there's no one on the main training field when you arrive. Just bring your boots and shin pads, ready for a game."

"Yes, yes," said Abebi excitedly. She was silent for a moment and seemed confused. "Sorry, is that all? Do I go back to my team now?"

"Ha ha, yes," said Suzie. "And can you send over Josie when you get there? I can see she's still there."

Abebi thanked them both, walking backwards as if she didn't want to take her eyes off them, before turning and jogging back to the group. Coach Ivan saw her coming and stopped mid-sentence, knowing that there would be another interruption that he would be unable to contain. Abebi walked up to Josie and told her to go across to where she'd been. Josie seemed reluctant to leave the group, but Abebi pushed her and some of their teammates urged her to hurry up. Abebi turned to Maya and grabbed her arms, widened her eyes and smiled. She felt hot and was blushing, even though no one would be able to tell that she was.

Coach Ivan's words weren't going in. He could have been singing a song for all she knew, and her mind was lost in a thousand thoughts, mainly nervy thoughts about what to expect at Tuesday night's training session and what she would say to her dad when they caught up at the dinner table.

Once the post-game analysis had been done and the players had done a half-hearted warm-down, Ivan called the three players across.

"So, you're going to Adelaide United on Tuesday night. We've had them watching our games ever since Maya joined our team, and they've identified all three of you as players for the future. I've given each one of you a good wrap. Don't let me down. Your names are known now, and you need to show what you can bring to their club as a person as well as a player. I believe in you. You've been playing so well this season, and you all deserve this opportunity. Be ready to shine."

They all fist-pumped their coach as they always did at the end of a game or a training session, and the girls walked over to their bags in silence, all processing the news in their own way.

Chapter 26

Feisty

Charles asked Abebi if she wanted him to be there for the trial. He was good at assessing the conditions when it came to navigating the treacherous terrain of raising teenage girls; with the trial only just around the corner, he wouldn't need to drop her there, but he made sure his daughter knew that he was happy to be involved. Abebi wanted him to be there and they made a plan to walk down together to Playford. Yetunde would come along too; her season with the local club team had come to an end a month ago and she had been earmarked by Abebi's club as a player they wanted to sign for their NPL youth program for the following season.

Yetunde was a totally different player to her sister. Without the early growth spurt that Abebi had gone through, she was altogether more compact, and had very quick feet and a shape and stance that screamed footballer. Abebi had been able to see her play a few times this season and was glowing of her little sister, who was altogether more feisty and busy, a real midfield terrier who pestered players, broke up attacks and could strike a ball with a lot of power. The talk around the dinner table on Sunday nights was only about football, and they compared stories and shared comments about the two games that day, as well as wrapping up the games they watched of the younger and older age groups that played before and after. On an ideal game day, Yetunde would play at 8.15 a.m., the first game of the day, and they would watch the first half of the next game before moving on to

Abebi's game. She had to meet at 10:30 a.m. for an 11:30 a.m. game. Charles would sometimes leave them to it after the Under 15s game, if he had something pressing to attend to, but sometimes he would stay the whole day and they would be there until the end of at least the reserve grade before it got too late.

Abebi loved the family feel of the club. The coaches and managers all seemed to be close; the parents had different roles, Charles happy to take an esky around the perimeter of the main field, selling cold drinks and enjoying the chats with the rest of the spectators and the banter with the opposing team's entourage.

"Special price for the visiting team," he would say, without specifying what the price was. He felt like he was back in Senegal, where a jolly, loud gentleman would do the same thing at the local football games. He was now the jolly, loud gentleman and he became quite well known for his singing and cackling as he ambled around the park towing his esky behind him.

Yetunde was destined to end up in the same talent pathway with Abebi; everyone knew her already, and she would kick the ball around with the other girls at half time in later games in the day. The question of money would inevitably be the hurdle, but Charles had already promised that he would give Yetunde the same opportunities that her big sister had.

Chapter 27

Shimmy

The Tuesday training session turned into a series of training sessions, all three Salisbury triallists invited to train on the Thursday and then again on the Saturday morning. That first session had seen them join a group of 16 young players from various clubs around the state, but by the Saturday morning there were only four of them left, including all three of the Salisbury players. The whole Adelaide United squad was there, the men and the women, and they were taking their team photos before training. The amount of fuss was unbelievable and the photographers were moving players around and asking some of the girls to change the way their hair was done in order to make the photos as aesthetic as possible.

This was eye-opening for Abebi. Josie and Maya were watching on in amazement too, all four remaining triallists mesmerised by the scene. Suzie and Ryan, the two officials they had met at their game two weeks previously, lined up for the women's squad. Suzie was a player, and Ryan was one of the coaches. The fact that they were both part of the first-team squad made Abebi's skin bristle. She was so close to what she wanted.

The training session that followed was like a dream. The four girls, the other girl a central defender with the mannerisms of a cowboy, trained with the first team. It was incredible. They had no idea that this was going to happen, and after the first half an hour of being unsure and following the lead of the older players in the warm-up, they settled into familiar drills that they had done all season with their NPL club. When the time came for a game, there were enough players for a full-field game—Abebi and Maya were in one team and had to put on a lightweight white shirt over their red training gear, while Josie lined up for the reds and they got straight into a game situation.

Being at the tail-end of the NPL season meant that Abebi was match fit. The first-team players were super-fit, most of them having played NPL too. Abebi felt like she was making her debut for Adelaide United. She was a picture of concentration, and every pass and every control of the ball was done with slightly exaggerated movement. She was making sure that she did the simple things correctly. When Josie sprinted towards her with the ball, and tried to shimmy past her, her long leg intercepted the ball and the red team were caught on the attack. The precise through ball through to Maya saw her advance on the goalkeeper, and whilst the first attempt was blocked, one of the first team players drilled the rebound into the unguarded net. Both Abebi and Maya received a lot of praise, and Abebi was amazed that everyone knew their names already.

Abebi was relieved when Josie tried her luck down the other side of the field and cut in to curl a shot into the bottom corner of the net. She would have hated to have spoiled her morning. The game ended as a draw, despite the coaches trying to fashion a winner by intercepting and laying on passes for the strikers, Maya smashing a fierce shot off the bar with the final kick of the game. All the triallists had been superb. Abebi caught her sister's eye as they walked off for a drink, and she was jumping and punching the air.

Suzie and Ryan called the four triallists in for a chat, Suzie doing the talking again. She was red in the face after marshalling the red team's defence for the past 30 minutes.

"Thanks for coming to training over the last three sessions. We've loved what you all bring to the squad. I'm making no promises, but the club will be in touch with you during the week to discuss where we go from here. Any questions?"

Josie cleared her throat.

"Are we being considered as players for this season's W-League?" she asked. That was the million-dollar question.

"Yes," said Suzie definitively. "Yes, you are. But like I say, we can make no promises to you right now. We have let the club know our thoughts and it is now up to the club to make decisions based upon what they have seen. You're all very young, and it is up to the club to decide what their policy with youth players will be going forward."

She was pointing her head towards the group of five or six people in black tracksuits, who were obviously the final decision-makers.

"They've been watching all of you this season, they've even watched videos of your games. Good luck and we'll hopefully see you all again very soon."

Suzie and Ryan traded fist pumps with the players. Abebi was totally star-struck. This was like a dream, a really exciting dream that would have left her trying to remember all the details when she woke up smiling.

School holidays had started and the final game of the NPL season brought Abebi and her teammates through to the awkward part of the year; the fabled retention letters had not been sent out yet and all the Salisbury Inter players were on tenterhooks until they knew what was happening for Under 16s next season. Abebi and Yetunde arranged to meet with some other girls from their respective teams to play football together in a park, miles away from home, but far enough away to make a day of it. This would become their go-to day out during school holidays, although the biggest day was the AFL Grand Final on the first weekend in October. The Adelaide teams would inevitably be knocked out early from the finals if they even made it that far, but the whole of Adelaide really came to a standstill on that Saturday. The girls all got together at Josie's house, where her dad Matthew and all the family made a massive day of it, with a lunchtime barbecue before the game, a big screen in the backyard for everyone to watch together and a continuation of the festivities into the night. One day the city would do this for the football, Abebi hoped, but for now this was a great way to spend the October long weekend, even though she still had no real grasp of the rules of Australia's national sport.

Chapter 28

Substitute

Abebi trotted out onto the field with her fellow substitutes and they took their place on the row of white plastic chairs that formed the makeshift bench. Charles and Yetunde were right behind them, Yetunde cheering with the other younger girls at the entrance to the tunnel. This Sunday afternoon pre-season fixture at the Marden Sports Complex had attracted a smattering of fans to add to the players' families and make at least some atmosphere on a hot day in late spring. Abebi was already glistening with sweat after the warm-up, but was now able to sit and take in the occasion—her first appearance on the Adelaide United team sheet.

The last few weeks had been incredible. Firstly, she was signed up by Salisbury Inter for next year's Under 16s squad, along with Josie. The next day, she received a call from Suzie on her new mobile phone to let her know that Adelaide United would be offering her a contract for the season to play in the W-League. She had kept her cool, walking away from the dinner table to get some privacy, before returning in a frenzied state when the realisation sunk in. Abebi slumped back in her seat. The completely one-sided conversation, Abebi only offering yes and no answers before ending with a "thank you", had her dad and her sister off their seats trying to listen in. When Abebi put the phone down on the table and looked up at Charles, he knew straight away and they all danced a jig around the room.

Abebi and Josie met with Adelaide United's Suzie and Ryan at Hindmarsh Stadium, and they sat in the main stand on the red seats, Charles and Josie's dad Matthew a few seats away, trying not to be excited, while still being part of the extended conversation. There was no paperwork; this was a question-and-answer session, and Josie was straight onto it. She had the confidence of someone who had negotiated such situations on a daily basis, and started the questioning, even though Suzie had said that she would explain everything first.

"Okay," said Suzie, interrupting. "Let's start at the beginning. You are being signed on a youth contract for the duration of the W-League season. That's not a long contract, but it covers pre-season games and either ends at the conclusion of the regular season or continues through the finals series if we make it that far. So that's 14 league games and a handful of pre-season fixtures, which start very soon."

"Will we get paid?" asked Josie. She looked at Abebi, who looked worried by the forthright questioning of her school friend and club teammate.

"Yes, you will be given an allowance for every game," replied Suzie. "It's not much, just over $100 each match you're involved in, plus an appearance fee of $100 if you play, plus reimbursement for any travel expenses."

Abebi was alert and alive. Being paid to play meant so much to her. Yetunde had been offered a place at Inter, but the question of fees had cast a shadow over it. Abebi made a pledge to herself at that moment that any money she received would be going towards her sister's fees for the season.

"Do we need to sign a contract or anything?" asked Josie.

"We'll get to that," said Suzie. "We have the contracts in the office ready to go. We'll sign those on the way out."

"Where's Maya?" asked Abebi, concerned that there were only two of them here today. Josie and Abebi didn't have any contact details for their younger teammate and were a little puzzled when they arrived and she wasn't with them.

"Ah yes, Maya," said Ryan, Suzie taking the cue to shuffle back in her chair and bite her lip. "Let's say her father wasn't happy that she would be playing through the summer months as they have a big holiday planned over Christmas and the school holidays. The family holiday won, and we won't be seeing Maya until next year."

Charles and Matthew looked at each other in surprise. This was the sort of opportunity that would warrant cancelling all holidays: an opportunity that may never present itself again. Abebi and Josie looked at each other in the same way, and then over to their fathers who offered nothing but a shrug of the shoulders. Suzie was almost grinding her teeth. This was obviously a sensitive topic. Abebi decided to get back on track.

"When is training? Does it clash with school?" she asked. She didn't care if it clashed with school or not, but was trying to sound as though school was just as important as playing in the W-League.

Suzie was back in the conversation.

"Most of our players have full-time jobs or are students themselves," she said. "Training will be very early morning on two days a week, away from the hottest part of the day, and we'll have one or two sessions at night. So no, you'll be able to go to school as normal."

Abebi slapped her thigh comically. They all smiled.

Josie continued to ask all the questions. How would they get to away games? Were they allowed to train with Inter? Would they be allowed to play in the school team? What would happen at the end of the season? Abebi sat and took it all in; she was loving Josie's persistent line of questioning, and knew a more delicate answer was required when Ryan spoke instead of Suzie.

Josie signed first and had a photo with Suzie, club captain and all-round Adelaide United legend, and while she was getting her photo, Abebi signed, still getting used to her signature. She had her photo taken with Suzie as Josie sat and beamed at her, and then Josie and Ryan joined the photo and the girls were given a shirt each to hold, making sure the sponsors names were front and centre. The dads were joking around by now, loving the fact that their daughters had realised a dream that was so far off in the distance only a few short weeks ago.

The players emerged from the tunnel to muted applause. This was potentially a low-key game, but for the two new recruits, both of whom were on the bench, this was the biggest football occasion they had ever experienced. Both players had expected to be sitting firmly on their white plastic chairs for the duration of the game, maybe doing some warming-up routines with the coaches to keep the real substitutes company, but Abebi hadn't counted on a head injury midway through the first half that saw the left back walk slowly from the field with blood all over her shirt. Immediately in the aftermath of the challenge, even before the physio was on the field assessing the damage, Abebi was told to warm up. Before she had really done any stretching, she was told to get ready to go on. The delay while the injured player was helped up and ultimately off allowed her to at least get some rudimentary stretches in before she was substituted onto the field. There was no player to high-five on the way off, no electronic board to show the numbers, just a pat on the back from the manager and some encouraging words from the players already on the field. Abebi had been an Adelaide United player for seven days and she was already in the first team.

Chapter 29

Contorted

Abebi sprung out of bed.

"I got paid! I got paid!" she yelled. "I've got money in my bank account!"

Yetunde was straight out of bed too and she peered over her big sister's shoulder as she scrolled through her internet banking account. She had only just had the account for three days, after visiting the bank with Josie and Josie's mum and of course her dad Charles, who had to be there to sign the application as the responsible adult. Abebi had never even contemplated having a bank account until then; after all, any work she had done so far in her life had been for cash. Doing letterbox drops for the local tradesmen, with their novelty fridge magnets and badly worded flyers, was only ever done for a note in the hand, and the refereeing she had done for the younger age groups was $15 in the hand when the club director was handing out payments to the referees of the youth NPL games. This was something new though, money in an account, and she had even received the bank card yesterday in the post and diligently signed the back of the card and visited the ATM to change her PIN.

"'Tunde," she said, grabbing her little sister by the hips and sitting her down next to her. "You know what this means?"

Yetunde looked excited and then almost as if she were going to break into tears.

"You're signing with Salisbury Inter!" she continued. "The Ngom family dynasty continues at Underdown Park."

She had slipped into a commentator's voice, and was pronouncing her words in the way Simon Hill would deliver in his eloquent manner.

"Next stop, Salisbury Inter Under 13s for Yetunde Ngom," she continued. "She's got big boots to fill, but the world is her oyster."

Yetunde jumped up and fell into a hug with Abebi, that turned into a playful wrestle and ended with Yetunde's head on Abebi's chest as they lay contemplating for a moment. One of them had to break the silence.

"Mum would be so happy," said Yetunde. "She would be so proud of you, Abebi. Playing football with the big girls, helping her sister follow in her footsteps."

They were silent again. Abebi's eyes misted over as thoughts of her mum's smiling face swirled through her head and almost before her eyes. She held on tight to Yetunde and couldn't speak, her cheeks forcing the corners of her mouth down and making it impossible to form any words. She could feel Yetunde's heartbeat and felt as close to her mum as she had for some time. It almost felt as though Yetunde was snuggling with her mum. Abebi slowly hummed Mum's melody that would always accompany moments like this.

The girls had been visited a few times by a friendly social worker lady who was also a family psychiatrist. She was great at putting them at ease and getting them to talk about their mother and they enjoyed the sessions. It had now been over a year since the last visit and the simple fact of not having an occasion to talk about their feelings meant that they were suppressed and ready to erupt at the right trigger.

"What would Mum be wearing today?" asked Abebi in the way that the psychiatrist would ask.

There was no rush for answers.

"She'd be wearing her 'boubou'," continued Abebi.

She could feel Yetunde's chest moving. She couldn't tell if it was giggling or crying until she raised her head and smiled through her moist eyes.

"The gold one," said Yetunde, staring into Abebi's eyes.

"It's Sunday morning," smiled Abebi. "Any respectable African lady will be up and dressed and ready for a busy day of meeting friends and drinking tea. After the markets, of course."

"Ha ha, yes," agreed Yetunde. "A big colourful basket of fruit and vegetables from the market. And flowers. Always flowers."

Yetunde placed her head on Abebi's chest again.

"Do you ever think about that man who pushed Mum into the road?" asked Abebi after a long pause had almost turned into a snooze.

Yetunde shot up straight and sat next to Abebi, who was surprised by the sudden movement.

"Yes," she said. "If I ever see him again, I don't know what I would do."

"Do you remember his face?" asked Abebi, knowing that his face was etched into her memory forever.

"He was tall …" Yetunde said unconvincingly. "He had really light hair and eyebrows."

"I know he had a cut underneath one of his eyebrows," said Abebi. "Although that might have been temporary. And I think he had a tattoo on the back of his hand. Like a star or something."

"A tall fair-haired man with tattoos: there can't be that many men who look like that in Adelaide," said Yetunde.

There was silence. Yetunde was wringing her hands. She was deep in thought.

"He killed Mum," said Yetunde after a while. "And I think I'd like to kill him."

"No, no," said Abebi, grabbing her by the shoulders. "No, don't think like that. What would happen if you killed someone? You'd be locked up forever, we'd have to visit you once a week and you'd never play football again."

"But he killed our mum," said Yetunde with pleading eyes. "He pushed her into the road and the bus hit her ..."

Yetunde's face contorted and tears dripped down her face.

"That's not fair," she said. "It's not fair."

Abebi sat with Yetunde in her arms, consoling her just like her mum would do if she was upset. They rocked slowly from side to side just like their mum would do with them, until Abebi started to talk about Salisbury Inter Under 13s again and football lightened the mood and Sunday morning got underway again.

Chapter 30

AFL

With the girls returning to school the next day and NPL football in recess, Adelaide United women's team was the focus for this Sunday, and Abebi had to report to training at midday for a 1 p.m. start. There were still a good three hours before she had to leave, and she flicked on the TV as the frying pan warmed up, ready to fry some eggs for breakfast. Charles had left before the sun had come up, manning his stall at the markets, and there was a note on the kitchen bench simply saying, "I love you both, love, Dad." There was little hope of seeing any football action on TV, with all the football now on pay TV, with Fox Sports showing the A-League games and Optus now in charge of the English Premier League. There was even less hope of her seeing her favourite team, Bolton Wanderers, in action, after their momentous slump into the fourth tier of English football had been cemented in May. Her Youri Djorkaeff number 13 shirt was looking the worse for wear these days, many shades away from white, and she would easily be forgiven for changing her allegiances; it didn't matter anyway, she couldn't watch the games, and she could only keep up with the scores by listening to the World Service on the big radio in the kitchen or seeing the scores when she could get on a computer at school.

Being a football fan in Australia was difficult. The days when the Premier League was on TV back home in Zambia, and they could all watch it during the day on the weekend, were where Abebi had learned to love football. Here in Adelaide, for the everyday sport-loving

Australian, there was little chance of exposure to football and that was why everyone followed the AFL. It was on TV all the time, it was on the news, in the newspapers, it was what all the boys talked about at school, even the ones who played football with her at lunchtime.

Sure enough, once the eggs were placed carefully on the toast, the yolks remaining intact, and the girls sat down at the table to eat, the TV channel still had AFL playing, despite the season having ended two weeks ago.

Chapter 31

Stealth

Adelaide United's W-League season had been going nowhere, without a win and only three points from three draws coming into the new year. That was until the name Abebi Ngom appeared in the starting line-up for the first time in a spirited draw at Canberra United on a hot January night in the nation's capital. With their American import Hayley Moreno returning home to rejoin her NWSL team and injury ruling out the regular left back Nikki Rafferty, Abebi's path into the starting line-up was surprisingly paved, and she remained there for the rest of the season.

An absolute thrashing of Western Sydney Wanderers saw Adelaide record their first win of the season a week later, Abebi setting up two goals from the left with her marauding runs and clever crosses into the danger zone. Further wins followed and the club sat poised for the finals by the end of the incredibly short season, when a run for the wooden spoon had looked nailed-on at the turn of the year. The guilty feeling of getting her chance before Josie was soothed in the final two games as her schoolmate came off the bench to play an important part in two exciting victories. But it was Abebi who was earning the plaudits, and she was thrilled.

The end of the season that saw them dumped out of the finals at the first hurdle by Melbourne Victory coincided with the dawn of a new NPL season, and the Salisbury Inter annual charity function was held the night after the Adelaide United end-of-season awards night.

The girls had really gone to town for the awards night, Abebi and Josie spending the afternoon getting ready at Josie's house before her dad dropped them at the swanky venue in town. Charles had picked the girls up well after midnight after a night of stardom and recognition that they could not have envisaged only a few months earlier. As a result, Abebi was a little jaded when the charity function came around, but Yetunde and Charles were buzzing. Charles was known by everyone at the club and there was a lot of fussing over Abebi. Yetunde seemed to be having the best time, mixing with her new teammates and enjoying the limelight of being the sister of a star footballer.

Abebi even got a mention in the speeches for her wonderful performances in the newly named A-League Women's and Charles and Yetunde were beaming at her as all eyes turned on her to see her reaction. Despite not being on top form, Abebi handled the situation well—after all, if she was going to be an Adelaide United player in future years, she would need to get used to the attention.

It was later in the night, as the music pumped and the dance floor rocked, that the evening took a strange twist.

"It's him, it's him," called Yetunde, eventually grabbing Abebi by the arm and frog-marching her through the doorway of the function room as an 80s Australian anthem had people heading the other way to the dance floor. Just off the hallway, on the way to the bathrooms, a man was sitting in the gaming lounge, engrossed or thoroughly apathetic at one of the pokies, the lights of the flashing gaming machine lighting up his face every few seconds as he pressed and pressed on the button. His face was in full view, but he would probably be unable to see past the sparkling lights that danced in front of him. He looked tall, despite being sat down. He had very light hair and matching eyebrows, and there appeared to be some sort of mark on the back of the hand that was impatiently drilling the button.

The two of them stood and watched, safe that the darkness of the hallway, the darkness of their skin, and the brightness of the lights in the gaming room would keep them out of his line of sight.

"That's him, isn't it?" asked Yetunde, pulling on Abebi's arm.

Abebi didn't want to believe it. She could feel her muscles tensing and she must have had a surge of adrenaline.

"Oh, that's got to be him," said Abebi in a low voice. She had entered a stealth-like state, her eyes transfixed on the target.

One of the young bar staff walked towards them, coming out from the gaming room carrying a tray of empty glasses and bottles. Abebi put out her arm as if she was going to hug him, but instead turned him around deftly with her arm and pointed with her head in the direction of the doorway where he'd emerged from.

"That man, there," she said. "What's his name?"

"That guy at the machine facing us?" asked the bartender. "That's Darius. Do you know him, do you?"

"I think I do," said Abebi mysteriously.

The young bartender looked at Abebi, whose face was very close to his, and she looked at him right in the eyes. This was the first time in her life that she had used her physicality to get what she wanted.

"Is it Darius McDonald?" she asked, her gaze piercing into his.

The bartender almost dropped the tray and had to catch it quickly with his other hand.

"D-Darius Jensen," he said, looking back into her unblinking eyes. "That's Darius Jensen, he lives out at Magill somewhere these days, but he used to live near here before. Always on the pokies. Tips well. Nice fella."

Abebi didn't know why he added that last comment, but she put her arm on his back and smiled, looking for a name badge and not finding one.

"Thank you, my friend," she said before he dashed away, no doubt thinking he'd just been in another one of the many drunken conversations that went on in the club on any given night, and his brain trying to remember the orders that he'd just taken from the night owls in the Prosperity Lounge.

Abebi was rattled. She had just acted like a gangster and she didn't like it. Her skin was fizzing and cold. Yetunde was staring, waiting for the next dramatic move; her sister had just achieved God-like status in her eyes and could do no wrong as they wandered slowly towards the main room. Charles broke away from the conversation he was having with a group of parents and let his daughters know that they would be leaving in 10 minutes.

"We're ready to go now," said Abebi.

"Oh, okay, let me just say goodbye to a few people," said Charles, surprised that the girls were keen to leave before the end of the party. He dashed off, but was soon caught up in conversation again, a fresh non-alcoholic beer in his hand. The girls split up and went to find their teammates to say goodbye and were back together while Charles was still chatting. The music eventually came to an end and was replaced by loud talking that subsided once people realised they didn't need to shout.

"Let's go," said Charles, with his car keys in his hand. "What are we waiting for?"

The car ride home was quiet. It was only 15 minutes at this time of night, and Charles gave up trying to spark conversation when he only got one-word replies. Yetunde passed her mobile phone to Abebi, with an Instagram profile up on the screen. Darius 'Bomber' Jensen was the name, Pro Wrestler. It was him all right. Abebi just passed it back without saying anything. She was still reeling from the way she acted back there. She had felt like her body had been possessed or that she had been watching herself on TV in a show about powerful women getting what they want. She was freaked out.

Chapter 32

Power

Training was getting intense with only two weeks of pre-season left, and both the Under 16s and the Under 13s SAP girls were now training. Yetunde was obviously making more friends at her school, and would go to training from school after spending time with her new group of mates. Abebi hadn't noticed her with any group of friends in particular, but they didn't exactly see much of each other anyway at school, the older kids keeping their distance from their underlings in the senior block.

The Tuesday before the new NPL season was due to start, Abebi was asked to arrive at training a little earlier as she had to meet a visitor. Coach Ivan, who had progressed to Under 16s to continue the development of what was a very talented team, either didn't know who it was or wasn't letting on who it was she was meeting. Abebi didn't mind secrets and surprises, and had forgotten all about it until her mobile phone alarm chimed in her pocket for a good minute as she filed out of school with the rest of the students before she noticed. She had brought her football gear to school and would be going straight from school herself to training. Yetunde was nowhere to be seen at the school gates and Abebi made her own way to training, catching the bus that ran along next to the school and walking the rest of the way. She had plenty of time anyway, and took her time, taking a different road in search of a shortcut that ended in a dead-end and she retraced her steps, giggling to herself.

When she arrived, coach Ivan was stood chatting with a lady in a blue tracksuit. As she got closer and they both looked to see who it was, she could tell it was a Football Australia tracksuit. Her heartbeat quickened and so did her stride. Her posture straightened and she now had purpose for the final 20 metres of the walk from the bus stop.

"Abebi, perfect timing," said Ivan, holding his fist up.

Abebi returned the fist-pump and offered a fist to the lady, which turned into a handshake.

"This is Dee. Dee Power. Of Football Australia," continued Ivan. "Dee has come to talk through an opportunity with you."

Ivan was like that. Never gave away a story if someone was going to tell it, but always giving away enough information to let you know if it was good or bad. He picked up the cones and bag of balls and walked over to where the first of the Under 12s and 13s were congregating. No sign of Yetunde there, but Abebi had other things on her mind.

Dee and Abebi walked over to the metal picnic table in the shade and took the cleanest end, the one without all the bird droppings. They sat face to face, which was surprisingly far apart. Dee went for small talk as an opener, asking Abebi how pre-season was going and about her season with Adelaide United.

"We'd like you to join the Junior Matildas for a training camp," said Dee suddenly. "The camp will be an opportunity for us to introduce new players to an extended squad and to play full-sided games with and against players of the same age and ability. Is that something that interests you?"

Abebi didn't hesitate.

"Wow, that's amazing," she said, a number of questions popping into her head about logistics and timing. She suppressed the questions and let her emotions lighten up her face. She was beaming.

"I'll confirm your position," said Dee with a broad smile that was simply a reaction to Abebi's delight. "The camp is in late March and we will fly you to Coolangatta and back. That's in Queensland. And you will be staying in camp on the Gold Coast with all the other girls. Have you been away from home before?"

That was quite a funny question, given where she had come from.

"This will be my first time," she said, hoping that would be the answer she was looking for. "It'll be an adventure!"

Dee was impressed at Abebi's maturity and her calmness, although the delight was written all over her face.

Ivan made a point of coming up to Abebi just before the warm-up started for training and gave her a knowing squeeze of the shoulders. Abebi hadn't mentioned the conversation she'd had with Dee to any of her teammates who had since arrived, and she saved her joy up for the car ride home, Charles having come to fetch both of them and having watched the last 30 minutes of Abebi's training with Yetunde on the sidelines with the rest of the parents.

"No way!" said Charles. "NO WAY!"

He was driving and couldn't take his eyes of the road. Abebi knew he would have been jumping. Yetunde was screaming in the back. Despite being the moody pre-teen, she loved being the little sister of a football star, probably because she knew her sister's success would help her own fledgling football career take shape. But mainly because she simply adored her big sister.

"Can I come?" asked Yetunde. "Can I, Dad?"

"Ha ha, let 'Bebi have her moment," laughed Charles. "We'll worry about that later."

Of course, Charles and Yetunde wouldn't be coming. The cost of the flights, the accommodation in a high-demand period, the time spent not earning and the fact that Yetunde was fresh at her new school were obvious reasons why Abebi would be going it alone.

"Where were you after school?" asked Abebi, turning to face her little sister, a calculated move to ask the question in front of their dad.

"I was with my friends," said Yetunde, who sat back and kept her stare as Abebi stared at her, looking for a flinch.

"Ah, okay," said Abebi. That was enough for Charles to be happy that Abebi's concern for her little sister had been quickly eased.

Chapter 33

Damage

The warm glow didn't leave Abebi for the next few days and she was so excited when Josie showed her the squad announcement on the Football Australia website when they were meant to be researching a history project on the school computers. It was for real. Her name was there, with a number of names that she didn't know and with a few that she did know from the A-League. Everyone would soon know, she figured, and she would need to keep her feet on the ground, with lots going on at school, NPL training and just the general busy-ness of life.

The next training session at Salisbury, Abebi offered to catch the bus straight from school with Yetunde, and Yetunde said she would check with her friends to see if they were meeting after school as usual. Abebi had concerns that Yetunde might be up to no good, but she couldn't quite put her finger on it. Her little sister was precocious but sometimes secretive, and Abebi tried to throw in questions on the bus ride and the long walk to training that might reveal what she was really up to. Yetunde was obviously very good at avoiding the tricky questions, or she was simply not up to anything at all.

Training was harder than usual. A couple of girls were sitting out with heavy colds, but Abebi was okay—she just felt a little jaded. She even made a few uncharacteristic mistakes during the small-sided game at the end, and put it down to her mind being elsewhere, her head already on the Gold Coast. Charles was chatting with a group of parents while Yetunde played with two other younger siblings on the adjacent field, and Abebi couldn't shake the faraway feeling, like she was in a dream watching herself going through the motions on the field.

"Baby, switch on!" came the cry from Josie as she was slow to react to a changeover in possession. That shook Abebi into life and when her opponent came racing down the line at pace, she was on her like a flash. Her opponent stepped cleverly inside, taking Abebi by surprise, and she reached out with her right leg to try and make the interception. She got her toe to the ball, her left leg giving way under the strain.

"Much better, Abebi," shouted Ryan as Abebi's team won back possession.

Abebi was on the ground. She'd felt a crunching sensation in her left knee as her foot slipped back and there was an intense pain now flooding to the outside of her knee, as if the blood being pumped through the area had thickened to the consistency of jam and was laced with a thousand tiny needles.

Her bloody-minded determination saw her try to jump to her feet, and she was upright by the time the ball came back to her side of the field, but when she put her left leg down to take off and join the action, she collapsed to the ground and grasped her knee tightly, letting out a yelp as she hit the hard turf. Play went on for a moment, but the players shouted at Ryan and play eventually stopped. The club physio, Carli, a tall young lady who was often at training and games mentoring the physio students doing their practical experience, broke away from her conversation and jogged onto the field.

Abebi was lying on her side and had just released her grasp from her knee and it felt like her letting go was letting it balloon in size. Carli gave a friendly smile, while Abebi's face was still contorted in pain, her eyes screwed up in anguish; she'd try and put Abebi at ease the best she could. The questioning started. Carli didn't touch her at all until she had been through a long list of questions, and then took her leg into her hands and felt up from the calf and then down from the quad.

The training game had ended prematurely and the rest of the players were off doing warm-down, with a couple, including Josie, staying with Abebi as she went through the initial assessment.

"Come on, we'll get you up and get you to the sideline," said Carli.

"It hurts so much," said Abebi, calmly but with an element of stress in her voice. "I don't think I can walk."

"That's okay, hang on," said Carli, who swept her up, cradling her in her arms and walking the 10 metres towards Charles, sitting her on one of the metal benches.

"What have I done?" asked Abebi. She was looking at Carli with pleading eyes.

"Well, it doesn't look like you've broken anything," said Carli with a faint smile. "I'd say there might be some damage inside the knee though, judging by how quickly it's swelling up."

There was muttering from the parents and Abebi heard the word ACL mentioned a couple of times. She didn't really know what an ACL injury meant, but she knew it was a big injury that she'd seen happen twice already in her time in the A-League. Abebi rested her head against Charles' arm and Yetunde held her hand as silent tears filled her eyes and rolled down her cheeks.

"I'll call your dad in the morning," said Carli. "We'll get you in to see someone as quick as we can."

Charles carried Abebi in his arms to the car and put her in the back seat. Yetunde took Abebi's place in the front seat. The car ride was silent, the absolute opposite from the last time they'd done the trip, apart from Yetunde's attempts to make small talk with her dad. Abebi thought it was either forced just to make light of a potentially serious situation, or she was immediately taking her spot as the footballer in the family. Whichever way, it didn't help the situation, and Abebi was stewing on the back seat in a treacle of heavy thoughts.

Yetunde helped Abebi take a shower. Abebi didn't have time to be shy, and sat forlornly on one of the plastic garden seats that Charles had placed in the shower recess. Abebi could reach everything, but when it came to touching anything below her left thigh, she winced in pain. Yetunde washed from her shin downwards, trying not to move the leg too much. She was as gentle as she could be and smiled at Abebi, a smile that was sent from her mum, and there was a flicker of a smile in return in recognition. Abebi knew straight away that she was in a difficult situation, but that those close to her would be there to support her.

Charles knocked and came in to tuck in his daughters, not something he would do every night, but tonight there was a need for extra care and love. He hugged Yetunde first and thanked her for being a great help tonight. He then came across to Abebi, on top of the covers with her leg lying on two spare pillows with a bag of frozen mixed vegetables that had been in the freezer for two years resting on top. He placed the extra blanket over her right leg and the rest of her body.

"What about the Gold Coast?" she asked, her hand on her chin.

"Don't worry about that now," said Charles. "We'll find out tomorrow when we go to the clinic."

"Have you heard anything?" asked Abebi hopefully.

"It's a bit late for that, I expect we'll hear in the morning," said Charles. "You sleep. If you need anything, you sing out. Like a bird. If it's like a cockatoo, I'll know it's serious."

They both smiled. Abebi closed her eyes; she was physically and mentally exhausted and even with a throbbing left knee, she was asleep in seconds.

Chapter 34

Insurance

"Yes, as predicted in your scan, you have a grade three rupture of your Anterior Cruciate Ligament," said Dr Erding. "The ligament is in two pieces and you will need surgery to replace the ligament with another tendon harvested from the same leg."

It sounded brutal. Abebi wasn't really concentrating. Charles did the talking.

"Is that the hamstring that you use?" asked Charles. He'd been looking online, diving into rabbit holes, after work yesterday and there appeared to be a few options. At least it was an educated question.

"Probably the patellar ... from the lower part of the knee," replied Dr Erding, looking impressed that Charles had a realistic query. "The tendon is just as strong as the hamstring, and, well, let's not disrupt the hamstring as well."

Abebi was installed on the couch. Charles had finally replaced the TV with a hand-me-down one that had a proper remote control, but Abebi's first interaction was to hit the power button to turn it off. She was struggling. Only a few weeks ago, she had been playing in the A-League, helping her resurgent team unexpectedly reach the finals. Only a few days ago she had been running around at training without a care in the world after being selected into camp with the junior national team. This didn't seem fair, but to Abebi, life had not exactly been a journey that flowed so far, and this was just another kink in the hose.

Abebi was lying on the couch as the world went on around her, and she tuned in to her dad's telephone conversations in the back garden. The TV was put on mute and she could make out most of the conversations. Charles obviously didn't want to have these conversations in front of his daughter.

"So, there is no insurance to cover the surgery? None at all?" asked Charles, incredulously. Abebi was off-contract at Adelaide United, and Salisbury's insurance was only for rehabilitation, and not for actual procedures themselves.

"I can't come up with that sort of money by Tuesday!" said Charles in a later conversation. He was exasperated and there was a loud noise as something had been launched a long way in the garden and hit the back fence.

"This is a player who has been selected to represent her country! How is there nothing you can do?" was the next line as exasperation turned into despair.

Charles came waltzing in with a smile on his face as though nothing was wrong. Abebi had hit unmute as he had walked in. He was doing a great job of hiding his frustration at what he perceived to be a totally unjust system.

Charles had explained to Abebi that they didn't have the money required to get the surgery. After all, it was a huge sum. The public hospital system would be a slow process, but he had already booked in an appointment with a specialist for three weeks' time, and even that was after a lot of cajoling and persistence. Abebi was fit enough to get up and start walking—and she made the decision to go back to school, Charles sourcing some forearm crutches to replace the ungainly and unsteady underarm crutches that she had been offered at her visit to the clinic. She felt that she had to get on with life, even though it felt as though her life had essentially ground to a halt.

The window for the surgery with Dr Erding had passed and there had been talk of a fundraiser at Salisbury to help Charles find the required funds for the operation. Being a proud man, he simply couldn't face the pity from the kind people at Salisbury Inter and immediately knocked it on the head. There had to be a better way, and he was indignant with those that told him that his daughter would be unable to play again without the treatment.

Abebi was a shell of the girl she had been two weeks ago. To say that football was a big part of her life would be a fair call, and with her one true passion whipped away from her, she felt at a crossroads in life. Did she replace that passion with something totally different, or did she do something about it? Could she help her Dad find the money? When she found out exactly how much she would need, it was almost like a lost cause, but she knew that she had to do it somehow. She rang Suzie from Adelaide United and they threw ideas around in a series of texts that day. Perhaps Adelaide could come up with some of the money, but it was still only a small fraction of the total. Recess and lunch were difficult at school. Josie had stopped playing at school, fearful of an injury herself, and they hung out in the library, strangely finding joy in getting their homework done before they got home at night.

Abebi's first time back at training was emotional. She had been dreading it, being the centre of attention for all the wrong reasons, but she was invited to join the talk at the beginning of the session, and the players got into a huddle without prompting. Josie gave a rousing speech as they linked arms in a circle. It was straight from the Alexandre Dumas book they had been studying for English.

"All for one and one for all," she said, quite the cheesy line, but delivered with the pomp that it deserved. She followed it up with a more thought-provoking "It is only the dead who do not return."

Abebi instantly felt like part of the family again, even though it would be at least 12 months until she could return to action. And that was if she could get the surgery she needed.

Meanwhile, Charles was on the sideline, waiting for Yetunde to finish her training and he seemed uncomfortable with the well wishes he was receiving from the other parents in Abebi's team. He was enduring as much torment as his daughter at not being able to provide her the one thing she needed.

Chapter 35

Benefactor

"Great news, Abebi," said Suzie. She had called five minutes before the bell was due to sound at school, and seemed excited. "We have the funds for your operation."

Abebi turned to look for a private spot to take the call.

"Are you serious?"

"Deadly serious," said Suzie, trying to play along with the gossipy teenage discourse. "We have received a donation from a benefactor who has asked us to co-ordinate your operation from beginning to end, as if you were an Adelaide United full-time player. You don't have to worry about a thing—Adelaide United will pick up all of your medical bills in relation to your knee operation, all the rehabilitation and return-to-fitness training you need. I'm so excited for you."

"Is this for real?" asked Abebi, still doubting every word she had heard.

"This is not a drill," said Suzie, continuing on Abebi's level.

"I don't know what to say," said Abebi. "Who would do such a kind thing?"

"I can't tell you," said Suzie, seeming to switch into a more defensive and professional tone. "They have requested anonymity. Let's just say that someone really believes in you, Abebi. A bank transfer was made from the Bendigo Bank to our bank today."

"Wow, I just cannot tell you how excited I am. I'm shaking right now ..." said Abebi and she could feel her emotions rising from her stomach and her mouth starting to quiver.

"Dr Erding will be in touch very soon with your dad and we'll get you back on the road to recovery."

"Thanks, Suzie," said Abebi with a hint of a sob. "You don't know what this means."

The bell had gone, phones had to be away, but she managed a sneaky text to her dad to tell him the news. She wanted him to know straight away as she knew he would be stressing so much and would be in a darker place than herself right now.

"This was a little more complicated than anticipated," came the words from Dr Erding when he came to see Abebi in her hospital bed post operation. These were words that didn't sit well with Abebi or her dad, and they looked at each other with fear in their eyes. "However, I'm happy to say that it was a complete success. There are two bone screws that will remain in your knee permanently, but they will cause you no symptoms."

Abebi's demeanour had gone from uptight to exhausted and she had slumped back on the elevated bed. Charles cracked a smile for the first time in a long while.

"So, when does the rehab start?" asked Charles, seeming to gloss over the fact that Dr Erding had spent a good five hours performing a miracle, and had backed it up with another operation on an elderly patient in between.

"We'll not make you do anything tonight," said the smiling doctor. "But be prepared to be up and walking in the morning."

Abebi had no notion of how painful her knee would be, and right now was enjoying a drip connected to a cannular in the back of her hand that contained something quite powerful to keep it far from her thoughts.

"When do we see you next?" asked Charles, thinking ahead.

"I'll look forward to your young daughter walking into the clinic next week," said Dr Erding, putting his hand on Charles' hand as if to reassure him that everything was going to be okay. "We'll have her back on the playing field soon."

Charles leapt to his feet and hugged the startled Dr Erding.

"Dad ..." said Abebi in a voice that suggested her detachment from reality due to the drugs as she reached out. "Not cool. Not cool."

It was morning. Charles hadn't returned to the hospital yet. Abebi had been awake for a good hour already after seemingly just getting to sleep a few minutes ago. The noises in the shared ward started early, way before sunrise, and breakfast was served at 6.30 a.m. when everyone seemed to be up and about. Abebi had shuffled to the bathroom during the night after asking the nurse how she would do it, with the cannula still attached and the drip on a trolley. But she managed, and had even put some weight on her knee to see what it felt like. Yetunde was first through the door of the ward, wearing her school uniform and looking left and right to seek out her big sister. When she saw her, she rushed over, her hands full.

"See what came for you?" she said, proudly showing off the bouquet of flowers. "And all of these too!"

She placed a pile of letters on the bed and gave Abebi a hug, still holding the flowers away from her body. Charles followed soon after, looking a little out of breath, and he dropped another letter on the pile.

"What's this?" asked Abebi, puzzled.

"I don't know," said Charles, leaning over and kissing Abebi on the forehead as she stared at one of the unopened envelopes. "The flowers had a message but it wasn't signed. These letters though, I've no idea ..."

She opened the first of the envelopes, the stamp an obscure Australian one, the postmark from the Northern Territory. It was a letter, and as she unfolded it, 20 dollars fell onto the bed. She read out loud.

"My dear Abebi, wishing you the best of luck with your rehab. We hope to see you back on the football field before long. Best wishes, Aicha, Zara and family."

"No way!" exclaimed Charles. "Do you know who that is?"

Abebi and Yetunde looked at him blankly.

"No?" he said incredulously. "Remember Aicha from the boat journey, the house next to the crocodiles, the red dirt garden?"

Yetunde shrugged.

"The boys who got us kicked out and taken to the police?"

Abebi's eyes lit up.

"Yes! Yes!" she said, sitting up. "Yes! She was the one who could fix anything. She fixed the air-conditioner that hadn't worked for 20 years."

"That's her," said Charles. "Your mum had kept in touch with a lot of our African friends, she was good like that. I found the address book and wrote to some of the names I remembered last year to tell them what had happened. Oh my."

Charles had tears rolling down his cheeks and he shuffled onto the bedside to give his daughters a tight embrace. The two girls had tears in their eyes too as they remembered their mum.

Abebi opened the next. It was from school, and when she opened the letter it showered little pieces of paper with dollar signs written on them. Her classmates had done a good job and Yetunde made sure she picked up every one of them.

"We can't offer any money," read Abedi, "but here's what it's like to be showered with cash."

She had an official letter from the school, a card from her teammates at Salisbury, and another handmade card that was from another family they had spent time with in the Northern Territory. Abebi felt happy. She felt that her mum was still with them and felt blessed that friends from that fantastic voyage all those years ago had kept in touch, thanks to her.

There were also two letters that were unsigned, both from Adelaide. One looked like Josie's writing and she may have got excited and forgot to put her name on, the other one simply signed off with an incomplete sentence that left her looking for more pages in the envelope. They were simple well wishes and she was so happy to have received them.

Later that day as she waited for the physiotherapist to arrive to begin her journey back to fitness, she reflected on who the mystery benefactor could have been. She was 50% sure that it was her dad and that he had somehow raised the money—she held her father in high esteem as he always seemed to get them through the tough times, but she couldn't quite see how he would have done it. It could have been Josie's parents too; they seemed comfortable in life, but still, that was a lot of money that they could have been using on their own costs with three kids. Was it someone from Adelaide United, or someone from the Junior Matildas? Probably not—they had already laid their cards on the table. Could it have been one of the extended African family who had been keeping in touch thanks to her mum? She even contemplated it being the man who pushed her mum under the bus that night on the way home, Darius 'Bomber' Jensen, but that thought made her tense up and get angry.

She had been surprised at how well her small family had coped since the loss of Mum. It was awful at the time, and Abebi just remembered going into mother mode for Yetunde and doing all she could for her little sister to keep her focus on the immediate things in life. The counselling sessions they had been offered were welcome, but all that did was take them back into the grieving stage and Abebi didn't find it practical or positive in any way. That wouldn't make the packed lunches and do the washing up at night, it wouldn't do their homework, it wouldn't keep Dad's mind on his work that paid the bills.

Not being exposed to any sort of mental health knowledge, she could well have been damaged goods now, but not knowing was probably better than knowing at this stage, and the practicalities of life would need to take precedence. Thinking back, Abebi and Yetunde had breezed through that incredible journey through jungle, across the ocean and into crocodile-infested Australia, and had treated it like a holiday. Maybe they were made of tough stuff. She had to be there for Yetunde too, and she had an inkling that she would need more guidance than herself through the choppy early teenage years. Being on crutches wouldn't help though, and being immobile, at least for the next week, could be the ingredient required to cultivate depression in the unstimulated mind.

Abebi lay back in her bed, the head of the bed raised at a 45 degree angle. At that moment in walked her physiotherapist with a jolly "hello" and any thoughts of sleep were eliminated immediately.

Chapter 36

Tackle

"You'll know when the time is right," said Carli.

Almost 12 months had passed since Abebi had injured herself and undergone surgery to repair her left knee. She had missed the entire Salisbury Inter season, sitting on the sideline until the last month of the season, when she could join the warm-ups and cool-downs at training. She had then missed the entire A-League Women's season, a season that was over in a flash anyway, running for barely four months and ending with Adelaide in second from last place. Not that she had been contracted with the Reds anyway, much to Charles' annoyance, but they had been instrumental in her return to fitness, and she was starting to turn some of the newfound curves back into muscle as the NPL season approached.

Josie had starred for Salisbury Inter last season, but the A-League seemed such a high step that she had still not made it past a few fleeting substitute appearances, and had not been able to show what she was capable of. Abebi was now preparing to play her first game since that long-term injury curtailed her career at what should have been the most exciting time. A low-key first run out in the new year saw the girls travel the short distance to take on Adelaide Olympic in the first 90-minute match of pre-season in the Under 18s. Abebi was understandably apprehensive after coming through six weeks of intense fitness training, and a series of rehabilitation sessions with Adelaide United that had left her aching but feeling alive.

"But should I just go in to a tackle, just to see what it's like?" asked Abebi.

"No, no," said Carli with a concerned look on her face. "If you think about it too much, you'll injure yourself. Just wait until the opportunity comes up; if there's a 50/50 ball that's there to be won and you think you might clash legs, just go for it. Your shin pads will help you, your size will be on your side and your knee will be stronger than anyone else's knee out there. Just don't force it. If it's 40/60, let it go."

Abebi couldn't grasp the conflicting advice and just let it wash over her. She was ready for a run-out, ready to see if match fitness really was a different beast to physical fitness, and there was a healthy crowd of parents and friends at Ferryden Park to welcome the girls back to action. Coming straight into the starting line-up didn't perturb her, and she was thrilled to have received the text showing her name in the starting eleven, somewhat of a Saturday ritual that she had missed over the past year.

The conditions were hot and the synthetic field was reflecting the heat. Abebi's feet were cooking in her turf boots. But she felt strong, she was looking forward to some jostling and shoving, and when the whistle went, she raced into the action, almost abandoning her left wing-back spot in favour of searching out the ball. Playing Under 18s for the first time was potentially daunting, but she was still one of the tallest on the field, and when she was forced into her first close encounter with her opposing winger, she didn't hesitate to drop the shoulder and shepherd the ball into touch with her opponent clambering on her back.

The moment she had been waiting for came midway through the first half. The same opponent had skipped past a challenge and was heading down the wing towards the byline. Abebi raced after her and just as she was catching her, threw herself into a tackle. It was the sort of tackle that makes the spectators wince when artificial turf is involved. She cleanly whipped the ball out of play, taking the player with her, who ended up on top of her. Abebi was quick to push her opponent off in order to get back on her feet, and the crowd roared with approval. Abebi Ngom was back. She had grazed a good patch of skin from her shin in the process and it was stinging like crazy, but the adrenaline pumping through her at that moment almost made her break out in a smile.

At half time, she walked into the changing rooms past Dee Power of Football Australia and stopped to shake her hand when she noticed. No time for chats though, they had a serious half-time talk and a lot of fluid to take on, so she trotted quickly down the tunnel to join her teammates. She was glassy-eyed with tiredness and squirted some water from her water bottle into her face.

"You feeling okay?" asked Ivan, conscious that she might be feeling the heat in such warm conditions.

"This is the best day of my life," said Abebi, quickly snapping out of her weary state and bouncing to her feet, shuffling from foot to foot like a boxer ready to step into the ring. The blood had started to dry on her weeping wound. It looked gruesome, but was a symbol of her return to action, and Abebi was loving it.

The second half was almost all Inter. Abebi started and finished a glorious move that saw her play two one-twos and continue her run into the box, where she was on hand to tap home when the goalkeeper could only parry the cross right into her path. As her teammates ran across to congratulate her, she could see what it meant to them, and was emotional by the time she arrived back at halfway ready to restart. Her fitness belied the conditions, and by the end of the game she had put in an incredible shift, eclipsing a lot of the girls who were meant to be fit but were coming back from a heavy holiday season of over-indulgence and sloth.

The final whistle saw the mainly red-faced players shake hands, and they made their way over to the sideline to grab their water bottles. Abebi's knee was stiff, as if it were reacting to the 90 minutes of changing direction and stop-start motion, but it felt strong. Her head was filled with happy thoughts, and even if some of the players didn't register that it was her first 90 minutes back in action, she was so delighted to be sharing the changing rooms with a winning team after a full game.

Dee collared Abebi when she finally made her way out of the changing rooms. The reserve-grade game was already underway, and they sat down on a bench to watch. Charles appeared and reached down for a hug, followed by Yetunde, who dived into Abebi's arms with delight.

"Dee, this is my dad Charles," she said almost apologetically, "and my sister Yetunde."

Dee stood up and shook both of their hands, before turning to Charles.

"We are going to ask your daughter to be part of our Young Matildas camp again this year," said Dee. "It's in Adelaide this year. Makes it easy for you."

"Ah, we were hoping for a holiday," quipped Charles without hesitation, remembering the conversation they'd had in the car the first time Abebi had been called up for the Junior Matildas camp. "Thank you for letting us know. It means a lot to us … a lot to 'Bebi."

Abebi's world had come full circle. She had taken a detour of approximately 12 months to arrive almost exactly where she had left off. The hard work and persistence that she had displayed throughout her rehabilitation had not gone unnoticed. After the reserve grade game, they decided to call it a day, and the car journey home was almost as excited as it had been a year ago, this time Charles and Yetunde jokingly planning what they were going to wear to the camp, when they were going to buy their Matildas shirts and which senior Matildas players they had to 'take out' to make space in the squad.

Chapter 37

System

As it turned out, the camp was more than a Young Matildas camp. With the Women's World Cup having recently been awarded to Australia in dramatic circumstances, this appeared to be the first step towards identifying the home-grown talent that would represent Australia in their home World Cup. It was a coming-together of all of the Australian-based players in the national teams' set-up. The Junior Matildas, the Young Matildas, the Under 23 Matildas and the Senior team all descended on Adelaide for a five-day camp. They played mixed games against each other. They played local teams who had not started their competitions yet. In the case of the older girls, they played against young boys' teams. That was always a challenge, the girls' teams never seeming to come out with any positives, win or lose.

The teams mixed together, training, doing fitness sessions, team bonding exercises, psychological sessions and eating together and it was a fabulous experience for Abebi. Her dad did turn up for one of the games with Yetunde, both decked out in their traditional African dress, colourful robes in gold and deep reds, which attracted the journalists present and put Abebi on the radar. Of course, Abebi didn't see it like that and was mortified when she spotted them. When Charles told her that it would have made her mum so happy, she was at peace with the situation.

One thing that Abebi noticed as the week progressed was the lack of depth on the left side. With superstar Daniella Gauchan, the resident left-sided player in the Matildas' senior team, and maybe the Under 23 winger Mandy Uhlenstall from Melbourne City, Abebi couldn't see any other left-sided defensive player across the grades, and that gave her a buzz, knowing that she could be third in line for a Matildas spot. It was, of course, clutching at straws. Coach Bernadette Bills may have had other ideas of repurposing players in different roles or changing formations, and a left-sided defensive player might not in fact be a requirement at all.

Abebi seemed to be the centre of attention at times on camp, coaches keen to speak with her about how she was feeling on her return to fitness and a lot of the media staff took a shine to her. She was even interviewed for the first time by a local journalist, who was more nervous than she was, even asking her at one point if she thought she would make the Socceroos team! All of a sudden, she felt like she belonged, she felt wanted and her performances on the field matched her mood. With her dad and sister watching, a mixed team of Australian players took on a senior team from Adelaide University and ruthlessly picked them apart. Abebi stormed up and down the flank. Her teammate, Anna Black, a much older girl on the right who had just come back from her own long-term injury, did much the same in a handsome victory with some incredible skill and goal-scoring feats.

The camp concluded with a meeting on the Saturday morning, before all the players headed back to their respective cities for the final pre-season weekend of NPL football. The roadmap for each of the teams was announced. The Junior Matildas would have a further camp towards the end of the NPL season, the Young Matildas would be heading to Costa Rica for the Under 20s World Cup. The Under 23s had a series of friendly games set up against new Under 23 teams from some of the big European nations and the Matildas would be preparing for next year's Women's World Cup with a series of difficult friendly games this year, before a trip to the United States next year and some ill-timed Asian Cup qualifiers leading up to the big event.

Abebi was absolutely thrilled; she seemed so close to making it, but she knew that she was so far away at the same time. Some of these girls had been in the system for years, and she was coming in fresh. She didn't even have a passport, and that was something that she noted mentally to discuss with Dad and with the team manager. Imagine being called up and not being able to travel.

Chapter 38

Championing

The form that Abebi showed in the NPL season was nothing short of outstanding. She was picked in the team of the week every other weekend and footage of her skill and pace were being shown on social media and on the Football South Australia channels. The footage would often be grainy, her dark skin often making her appear from nowhere into the bright floodlights, but her unbelievable athleticism was plain to see. She wasn't even the tallest in her team now, Salisbury having signed a giant central defender, but when her legs were stretching out in a sprint, she glided across the turf and breezed past players with her speed.

Inter reached the finals, so the season was prolonged into late September, and the Grand Final day marked an amazing achievement, despite a sending off and a 3–1 loss to the Adelaide United youth team. The fact that they had made the Grand Final was amazing, considering they had knocked off the premiers in the semi-finals, Abebi scoring twice in a narrow win. Playing against players who she had trained with for the last two seasons at Adelaide United, and who she was having regular sessions with as the new A-League season approached, was a thrill, Abebi's insight into the opponents paying dividends when she advised her goalkeeper to stay central when facing a penalty and she made the save look easy.

Abebi had attracted interest from elsewhere too, Perth Glory all but offering her a contract for the 2022/23 season back in August, but she was keen to see what Adelaide United were offering first, and she was conscious that living away from the family would be a difficult ask. She loved talking with her dad about it, and Charles loved that she was so open about what her thoughts were.

"You can go to Perth," he said when hearing the doubt in her voice. "We will support you from afar and we'll make it a big event when you come to play Adelaide United."

That changed when she showed an interest.

"You know, Yetunde needs you here right now," he said with a stony face that even Abebi couldn't read. "Let's have a word with the Adelaide people and let them know about your offer from Perth."

Little did Abebi realise, but her dad was quite the businessman, a master at creating demand for goods and skilful at manufacturing interest where there was little interest before. He was straight on the phone with a journalist he had got to know and let some of the news slide out during a very jolly conversation, Charles playing the part of soccer dad very well while feigning to ask for advice. Abebi sat in wonder at her dad's brain whirring after every sentence the journalist said, and marvelled at his responses. By the end of the five-minute call, Abebi was sure that the journalist would be straight online to post about how Abebi Ngom was rumoured to be heading to a club in the A-League Women's, and when she checked online later that evening, sure enough, there was an article on the Impact Women's Football website about the player drain from South Australia, Abebi's rumoured move to Perth the headline.

Adelaide United were caught unaware and Charles received two calls from NPL clubs in NSW the following day, enquiring as to Abebi's plans, before Ryan from Adelaide United called and quickly started discussing terms for a new contract. Charles had become a football agent to his daughter without knowing it, and Abebi was signed up to play for United even before her NPL team had reached the finals series, and on very attractive terms. Josie was so excited to see Abebi at the next training session, both of them having been re-signed for the new A-League season, and there was more exciting news as teammate Maya was added to the roster too.

A by-product of Abebi's success was that her sister Yetunde was getting additional attention too. She had been playing for Inter for some time now, and even before the end of the latest season, as Abebi was tying up her A-League contract, Yetunde found herself training with other clubs in the area. The forward-thinking Adelaide Olympic, relatively new to women's football and offering free registration to all women players, were assembling very strong squads ahead of the trial season and Yetunde received an offer to join their talented Under 16s team for next year. This was obviously done quietly, given that the current season was still going ahead and that the trial season hadn't officially opened yet, but Charles ran through the scenarios with his two daughters and they made the decision that Yetunde would join Olympic for the following season. With Abebi part of the furniture at Inter, this would present some logistical difficulties, getting both of them to different venues on potentially different days of the week, but it would give Yetunde the best possible chance of following in her sister's footsteps.

It was an awkward end of season for Yetunde; she thanked Salisbury Inter for their offer of retention before receiving an award at presentation night. Two days later she politely declined and Yetunde signed for Adelaide Olympic, the same journalist somehow getting wind of the change and an article appeared in the local press championing the dawn of a new era for women's football at Olympic.

Chapter 39

Sacramento

Abebi's Adelaide United season had started well, the women's game finally getting its moment in the sun in Australia when the A-League Men's season paused for the controversially timed FIFA World Cup in Qatar. It coincided with a dream run for the Socceroos though and all eyes were on the Middle East when they should have been on the local women's competition. The short break over Christmas, where Abebi had driven up to Port Arthur to the holiday shack with her L-plates proudly on display, was now a distant memory and Adelaide United were trying to arrest an alarming slide down the ladder. The Women's World Cup was starting to enter the consciousness of every female footballer, but it was still half a year away. Charles had taken Abebi and Yetunde into the local post office to get their photos taken for passports, which Abebi thought was very unusual. Was her own dad keeping secrets from her? She even had to sign her name for her passport application, so it was very real.

It was January 10 and training was in full flow. An intense but thoroughly enjoyable fitness session was suddenly interrupted as a group of players and staff burst out noisily onto the field. Abebi stopped and put her hands on her hips. This was odd. Josie, who had been nursing a hamstring injury and was only just getting back to running, led the group who raced towards Abebi, rushing in for the hug before the rest of the group reached in to congratulate her. Abebi stood there like a player who had just scored against their childhood team, but she was genuinely nonplussed.

"Ohhh, let's go Matildas, ohhh let's go Matildas," chanted the group. Abebi realised what had just happened. She had just been selected into the national team squad for a tour of the United States at the end of the month—she should have remembered that the announcement was today. After all, she was just speaking with Dee from Football Australia yesterday who was checking to see if her passport application was underway. Now that realisation had set in, Abebi joined the jumping around and had the broadest smile on her face. Training was curtailed, and the rest of the team followed the celebrating mob back into the main building. The TV that had been paused was rewound to the moment when coach Bernadette Bills read out number 46, Abebi Ngom, even managing to get the pronunciation correct, and the whole room erupted again, all eyes on Abebi, who had her hands on her face and had a tear in her eye.

This was a two-game series in the United States, one game in Los Angeles against Mexico and one game in Sacramento against Canada, and that second game most likely to be the one where Abebi would figure, being against effectively Canada's Under 23 team. Abebi had not picked up on the somewhat unsubtle hints from Dee the other day on the phone, but it all made sense now. The left-back spot, owned by Daniella Gauchan, a powerful left-footed player who had recently moved back to the A-League with Western Sydney Wanderers, had been a problem for the Matildas for a few years, very little in the way of cover coming through the ranks. Abebi's standout year in the NPL and the terrific start to the A-League season had seen her catapulted into contention as cover for Gauchan; her sparkling performances going forward had given an extra dimension that was deemed attractive enough to bring her into the full national squad.

The Adelaide players were ushered back onto the field and Abebi followed, only for Ryan to stop her at the door and instruct her to get showered and changed, check in with her family and be ready for a first interview as a Matildas player.

"You knew!" exclaimed Abebi when she returned her dad's missed call. "How did you know?"

"I didn't know 'Bebi," said Charles calmly, with a hint of a laugh in his voice. "I just had a very good feeling. Congratulations to my beautiful girl."

"I'll call you back later ..." said Abebi after a pause, unable to hold it in. Her mum had always called her 'beautiful girl' and that triggered an outpouring of emotion, and she was in floods of tears as she showered, the water washing those tears away to the point that she felt like a different person when she eventually turned the water off with a shudder of the pipes. A quick check in the mirror, and she couldn't tell that she had been crying only minutes ago. She was a Matilda now, there were people already waiting to speak with her about it, and it felt as though she had matured five years in the time it took to change into her Adelaide United tracksuit.

Chapter 40

Passport

A TV camera was in place on a raised platform at the back of the makeshift press conference room at the front of the main building of the Adelaide United training centre. There were five or six rows of seats in front of it, facing a desk, itself on a raised stage. The desk had Adelaide United and Football SA signage on the front side to hide the legs of those being interviewed and there were bottles of water and microphones on the desk. This was incredible. She had been in rooms like this previously after Adelaide United games, taking an interest in how it all worked, but this was all for her. Aside from the cameraman and his assistant who was obsessed with the health and safety hazard of the long cables running across the floor, the room was empty. Abebi stepped in with Anthony, the club media officer. He was the epitome of cool, contrasted with the nervous bundle that was Abebi, her posture one of a young teenage girl being presented with an award at school, shoulders cocooning her arms and head slightly bowed.

"Abebi," said Anthony. He had stopped her in her tracks as they walked over to the desk and turned to put his hands on her shoulders, looking her straight in the eyes. "This is your big day. Relax and enjoy it. If you think you're nervous, think about those journalists who'll be here in the next 10 minutes. They're all on edge, not knowing who's going to run their story and where their next paid gig is coming from. We're in charge of the room. You answer the questions that you feel comfortable with, I'll jump in if you get stuck."

Abebi was looking at him square in the eyes, not knowing what to make of it all. Anthony pinched her shoulders and pushed them back.

"Be confident," continued the savvy media man. "You're a beautiful girl with the world at her feet. You can't fail here, just be yourself."

Abebi smiled and widened her eyes. She picked Anthony's hands off her shoulders, her posture staying in place, and made her way over to the desk, carefully negotiating the step, and took her spot at the furthest end of the table.

"Abebi, you're in the middle," said Anthony with a look of incredulity on his face. "This is all about you."

Abebi stood up, pushed the chair back in and moved to the middle chair. Anthony remained in the middle of the room and walked over to one of the seats that were for the journalists.

"Feel comfortable?" he asked.

Abebi still hadn't said a word, but looked a picture of calm, almost regal in her confident pose.

"Anthony," she said with a dramatic pause. "You'd better get used to this. I'm going to be a star."

Whether she meant the star of the press conference, or a star on the field for the Matildas, it didn't matter. Abebi had already been involved in a handful of team sessions where a public relations expert had run them through the process for pre- and post-match interviews, but this was quite specialised and was 100% about her. She handled herself impeccably; her nondescript, almost forced clear English accent gave her an air of command of the room. The way she avoided football clichés and talked with authority without any awkward stumbles and without diverting her eyes from whichever journalist asked her a question made her instantly likeable. Anthony grabbed her around the shoulder again as they walked back to the changing rooms, this time as if they were walking home from the pub at 3 a.m. after a family reunion.

"Abebi, that was awesome," he said sincerely. "We have the Matildas' next superstar in our midst. People will be talking about you as soon as this hits the airwaves. Interesting question about your eligibility to play for other countries too. You do have an Australian passport, don't you?"

Abebi looked at Anthony and smiled.

"Of course I do."

And of course she didn't, at least not yet. Who knew what the Australian passport office would think when they processed an application of a Senegalese girl with four first names and a surname that sounded Vietnamese, who had lived half of her life in Zambia and had magically appeared in Australia, being granted permanent residency as a refugee and living in Adelaide's north. Red flags and police checks for everyone!

She was straight on the phone once she had picked up her bag from the dressing room, ignoring the long list of messages and alerts to ring her dad.

"I do have citizenship, right?" she blurted out when Charles answered.

"Of course you do, 'Bebi," came the answer. "Remember the paperwork we had to fill in for your driving licence application? They wouldn't give it to you if you didn't."

Abebi wasn't convinced even though her dad sounded more than convincing. She had visions of Charles fretting about his daughter not having her passport yet, making multiple visits to the passport office on Currie Street in his suit and sweet-talking his way into a meeting to get her passport. She wasn't going to worry about it now though. If her dad said it was all okay, then it was all okay.

Chapter 41

Envelope

When Abebi received a call from Dee two days before she was due to fly to Sydney to meet up with the Matildas team to fly to the U.S., asking for her passport number, she was sure that she would have to let her know that she didn't have one. She had hounded Charles about it since the announcement, but he had assured her that the passport was ready and that he 'just had to find time to pick it up'. When she was dropped back home later that day after training by her teammate who lived further up the road, she was ready to confront her dad. Cool, calm Abebi transformed into raging hot Abebi in the time it took to walk up the driveway and into the house, her impatient wrangling of the lock and the handle underlining her readiness for an encounter. What she found when she arrived though was a smiling Yetunde, sitting at the table with Charles, in his only suit, surrounded by paperwork, admiring her shiny new passport.

Abebi's demeanour had reverted back to the cool, composed girl everyone knew. She did a U-turn, kissed her fingers and touched the photo of her mum next to the front door. She returned with a smile and pulled out a seat next to her dad. His glasses were perched on his nose and he was reading through a letter, his head tilted backwards, while Yetunde sat back with a big grin on her face and stared at the photo page in her passport. After an uncomfortable moment when the seeds of doubt were sown once more, just as Abebi was going to say something, and without diverting his gaze from the letter that he was clearly just about to finish, Charles lifted up an envelope and slid out two more passports that thudded onto the table.

Abebi grabbed them almost before they hit the table. The years of playing cards on this very table had sharpened her reflexes. She instinctively picked the correct one, flicking the pages of the stiff booklet until the thick plastic page opened at her photo. She marvelled at the patterns swirling across her face. The photo looked startlingly like her mum. She looked at Charles, who had finished reading and was looking at her.

"You do look like your mum, you know," said Charles knowingly, putting his hand on his eldest daughter's arm.

Yetunde leaned in to have a look and Abebi had tears streaming down her face. What she would give for her mum to be here, living these incredible moments with her family. Charles and Yetunde were reading her mind, it seemed, and Charles put his arm around Abebi and pulled her in for a cuddle, the three of them rocking slowly in an embrace while they all thought about their loved one.

Abebi picked up her mobile phone and dialled the number she had for Dee, slowly extracting herself from the family hug.

"Great, thanks, I have the passport number," she said, before reading the passport number out twice and listening for the confirmation. Dee was clearly relieved, and wished Abebi a safe flight to Sydney.

Chapter 42

Reclaim

Abebi was by now quite experienced at catching flights, but they had all been as an entourage so far and she had let the club representatives take care of the check-in process while she goofed around with her teammates. She had missed the trip to Wellington Phoenix last season as it clashed with an exam at school, and she hadn't even registered that the club hadn't tried to get her an exemption for the exam. She wouldn't have been able to go anyway without a passport. This was her first time at the check-in where she was the solo traveller and she was the one out of the group who had a vague idea of what the process was. Charles happily took the backseat and let Abebi do the check-in process on her own at the kiosk and Yetunde then wheeled her Football Australia-branded suitcase over to baggage drop where they were helped by one of the customer service team, Abebi's blue tracksuit with the Australian crest receiving knowing looks and smiles.

This was only a short flight to Sydney, where she would be met by someone at domestic arrivals and driven over to the international terminal to meet up with the rest of the squad. Yetunde was the first to hug her sister, and Charles left her with a long hug goodbye before she joined the line for security and her family rushed off to minimise the parking cost.

Arriving at Sydney Airport after sitting at the front of the plane in business class, Abebi was one of the first off the flight, and the Football

Australia representative was indeed there to meet her as soon as she emerged from the aero bridge. The well-dressed middle-aged man with a clipboard took her hand luggage and they made their way down the long wide corridor making small talk, down to the baggage reclaim. This area of the airport always puzzled her—couldn't someone just come in off the street and steal her bag? Those initial moments of doubt when the first bags come through with no sign of hers was only short-lived, the branded suitcase appearing, splashed with rain, on the conveyor belt. Her chaperone leapt to grab the suitcase off the carousel before Abebi could react, and they were quickly on their way to the station down below to catch the train to the international terminal.

Abebi was loving it. She had the five-star treatment from her personal assistant, Mark, who produced the necessary ticket from his pocket to get her through the barrier as he went through the oversize barrier with her suitcase. The premier experience continued as they arrived at the international terminal and he led her to the fast-pass gate for security and they went through the security queue right to the front. A young girl raced up to her as she collected her belongings at the other end and asked her for a photo.

"You're Abebi, aren't you?" she asked. She was only nine or ten.

"Yes! Yes, I am," said Abebi before asking instinctively, "and what's your name?"

"I'm Alessia. You play for Adelaide United! Can I get a photo?"

"Of course!" Abebi was shocked. This was the first time she had been recognised outside of Adelaide and outside the context of a football stadium. How far had women's football come when a young girl in Sydney knew who she was!

Mark smiled and nodded as if to give approval for her to spend the time taking the photo, and she had a few words with Alessia's mum and dad, who were beaming, if not a little puzzled by their daughter's detective work.

Mark held his hand out as if to suggest they should be on their way, but his smile was as big as Abebi's. This must have been a fantastic moment for the Matildas' new squad member, and Abebi recognised that Mark must have felt like a proud father.

They went up a level on an escalator and through a private but inviting double doorway to the Qantas international first-class lounge. They walked straight past the concierge and turned the corner to see players excitedly greeting each other. Abebi spotted Mandy Uhlenstall and Anna Black from Melbourne City, who had just arrived and were working the room, giving out hugs and hand clasps. Mark introduced Abebi immediately to Bernadette Bills, the Matildas' head coach; they had talked on a zoom call a few days ago, but this was the first time they had officially met face to face. Bernie knew that she would need to be introduced to everyone, and she took the time to follow the Melbourne City girls and present Abebi to her new teammates. Abebi knew most of them by sight, if not by name, but there were some faces, mostly the coaching, media and physio entourage, that she didn't know at all.

There was no time to be nervous. It felt normal, and she was embracing being involved in the Matildas squad as if it were a natural progression, like a new year at school. The first-class flight to Los Angeles was something else. Abebi had to be briefed about how first-class travel worked, and she felt like Mr Bean as she sat in her seat and fiddled with everything to adjust her seat, checked out the private fridge next to her, rifled through the pouch that contained an array of cosmetics and chatted excitedly with the head physio, Nina Josifoski, in the pod next to her.

"We can have all of this?" she asked, astonished.

"Ha ha, of course," said Nina. "I'll be watching you like a hawk though."

The temptation was there to stuff her face, and her pockets, imagining Yetunde's face if she came home with skin toner, hand moisturiser and Belgian chocolates. It wasn't long into the flight though before she was completely at ease, and the coaching staff and physios began to use the flight as a fact-finding mission to assess the fitness of their playing roster.

Chapter 43

Questions

The two-game series in the U.S. was a total blast for Abebi. Even though she didn't play at all in the two games, not even in the second game against a weak Canada team, she was involved intensely in training and was treated exactly the same as the rest of the squad. From all the lists she had seen, she was officially a train-on player, but was still listed on the team sheet and was kitted up with a high-numbered shirt with no name. Just being involved was enough for Abebi; it might even have been overwhelming to have to actually play, especially in the first game against Mexico in front of a huge crowd. The highlight of the night though was joining the LA Galaxy home fans for the MLS game, the main drawcard of an incredible double-header, and Abebi felt right at home amongst the crowd cheering on from the cheap seats.

Mixing with global superstars such as Joelle Martins of Chelsea and Paris St Germain's Pia Nicholls was incredible. Just being in their presence, seeing how they interacted with their teammates, how they trained and prepared for games was fascinating to Abebi. She found herself asking so many questions, and no question was too stupid, even if some of the questions were met with a smile.

"How do you communicate with your non-English speaking teammates?"

"Why do you press so high into the player's back?"

"What are those shin pads? They're so small!"

"How come the refs don't penalise you for having your hands on your player?"

"Why don't you warm down like everyone else?"

Abebi didn't even notice that she was asking so many questions, and she was impressed at how open and patient her squad mates were in answering every one of them. She was conscious not to ask the same question twice, but asked them differently if she hadn't got the answer she needed.

The trip to the States culminated in the team gathering to watch the final qualifying game for the Women's World Cup on TV, South Korea finally securing their spot in the upcoming tournament in Australia and New Zealand with an unconvincing win against lowly India. The hype for the World Cup was starting. It was very real now, and when the squad returned to Sydney, they were transported to the Intercontinental Hotel for a formal event to view the World Cup draw taking place in New Zealand.

Australia were drawn in a group with a powerful-looking Spain, outsiders Scotland and unknowns Colombia. The players were all interviewed before and after the draw, and the best moment was Brisbane Roar's Scottish-Australian Michael Stewart jumping to her feet when Scotland's ball was drawn out of the goldfish bowl. Her teammates jumped on her in celebration and it made great TV for the Australian football public. The FIFA juggernaut was coming to Australia.

Stepping out of the plane at Adelaide airport and into the terminal gave Abebi a sense of deflation and elation in equal measures. The adventure in the United States was over, the excitement in the lead-up to the trip was instantly replaced with a feeling of 'what next?' and it felt overwhelming. At the same time, she was thrilled to see Dad and Yetunde as she walked through into the baggage reclaim. They were both smiling from ear to ear and Yetunde rushed up for a hug. Abebi looked her in the eyes for a moment then held her tight, the fleeting feeling of meeting a stranger replaced with a flood of emotion as she bonded again with her sister. Charles joined the hug and kissed both his daughters on the head. Abebi didn't want to let go. It was great to be back with her family.

Chapter 44

Gutsy

There was no rest from that moment. The NPL season was in full preparation mode for the new season and Salisbury Inter had a game the following day; Abebi was insistent that she would attend training that night to stake her claim for a place in the team. After all, she hadn't played a real game for two weeks and was raring to go after rubbing shoulders with Australia's football elite. She felt a stride quicker than she had before, a few centimetres taller, as if her Inter teammates had been stuck in a time warp. Her touch was incredible and her concentration levels were at a new high. In the short full-sided game at the end of training she found herself trusting her teammates more and she secretly hoped that they would rise to the levels of the training she had been part of in the U.S.

Adelaide United had picked up a win and a draw in Abebi's absence, and as a result were an outside chance of making the finals series, albeit with quite a combination of results required in the final two games to make that a reality. The crossover of A-League season to NPL season was notoriously difficult to manage for all the players involved in both. Abebi knew that the A-League was where she would be noticed; they paid her more money than she had ever earned and the quality of the players was next level, but the NPL was exciting. It was where she could shine and take advantage of sometimes being the strongest and fastest player on the park. With United having a bye this weekend, she was free to play and she could also play the next game, a midweek game that didn't clash with A-League training.

Pre-season continued for the next month, training two of the three sessions a week with Salisbury, the other two midweek nights with Adelaide United, and an NPL pre-season game or an A-League game on the weekend. The autumn storms rolled through, causing havoc to the Salisbury schedule, but Adelaide United trained and played regardless of the conditions. The Matildas fell further from Abebi's thoughts, with no additional games being scheduled until just before the World Cup, when the unfortunate timing of the Asian Cup qualifiers would take the Australian national team to the Middle East and Vietnam. Abebi was enjoying a lot of additional attention, local and national media outlets keen to get the lowdown on the latest addition to the Matildas camp, even though she was still only officially a train-on player. Fledgling football website Codyo Sports took special interest in her and they flew a reporter out from Sydney to interview her at the Salisbury training ground the day before she starred in a big win for Adelaide against Brisbane Roar. Abebi felt special, more so when the same reporter collared her after the match for another interview, and it was a feeling that would intensify as more media commitments saw her increasingly tied to her mobile phone.

Adelaide United's season ended with a gutsy draw in Melbourne against Western United, the hosts preventing Adelaide from moving up a spot in the table, both teams ending up towards the bottom of the table, but still with an air of respectability. The final day of the A-League season was teed up for terrific drama, and the players were invited to spend the following afternoon together in an upmarket part of Adelaide at one of the club director's house. It was billed as a celebration of the end of the season, but everyone was eager to take in the action on TV that would see one of three possible contenders to the crown take out the premiership. Abebi watched on in awe as Melbourne City, with two of her Matildas squad mates, won the league. Anna Black scored the deciding goal at the end of the game at CommBank Stadium, racing to the small pocket of fans in the corner to celebrate in style. They had been the best team all year.

The game over and the TV no longer the focus, more people arrived including members of the men's team, and the vibe went from formal event to party in a short period of time. Abebi hung with the youngsters in the squad, and they quickly became the centre of attention from the youngsters in the men's squad. There was a lot of laughter and flirting. Abebi had never been in this sort of environment and didn't know how to act—she remained calm and reserved as some of the boys drank beers and acted the fool. This seemed like a coming of age almost— it was only a year ago that she would have been hanging outside at a social event acting like a young awkward teenager, and now here she was acting sophisticated at a million-dollar house in the middle of Adelaide. She was relieved to have heeded the advice to dress more 'going out' than 'winding down' and she felt confident in the flowing dress that she had bought at the Vinnies store a few weeks ago on a shopping expedition with Josie, with this kind of event in mind.

One of the older Adelaide men's players came over and introduced himself. He was a tall defender and she knew him, Harry, from her days at Coopers Stadium supporting the men. He wasn't old, just a little older than the young boys who were goofing around. And he was tall, taller than herself. She would have a photo of them together as player and fan in her phone from a couple of years ago.

"Tell me, Abebi," he said, nailing her name, "how was your time in America?"

That was enough to get Abebi talking, and Harry hung on her every word, asking more and more questions to find out more. Abebi realised that she had been talking about herself for the last half an hour and tactfully turned the conversation.

"You've played for the junior national teams, haven't you?" she asked, knowing full well that he had represented Australia at Under 17 level. She was getting the hang of this, and she found herself touching her hair and looking at his mouth even though she was consciously trying to avoid it.

They were locked in conversation and she loved it. It was this easy talking to men. Why did her friends make it sound so difficult? Abebi was quickly becoming a woman, and with the step up in professionalism with Adelaide United and with the national squad, with media commitments and increased interest in her as a person as well as a player, she seemed to grow up another five years in a matter of weeks.

Chapter 45

Assembly

The Matildas squad announcement was in two stages. The NPL season was well underway, Abebi enjoying a stellar start, even getting on the scoresheet twice, and it was no surprise when she received the call from Matildas head coach Bernie Bills the day before the preliminary squad announcement. In retrospect she would have preferred not to know, as she was under strict instruction not to tell anyone outside her close family. In the end, she had training only an hour later and she made the conscious decision to tell no one at all, not even her dad or her sister.

Abebi had a feeling that something was up when she arrived at school the next day and was called into the hall early for morning assembly. This was her final year of schooling and it had already been interrupted, but the school had been very good to her, offering remote sessions with her teachers and giving her work that she could take away and do in her own time. Her grades had never been outstanding, and in some subjects she had been downright awful in the past, but a shrewd selection of subjects for Year 12, including taking French, a subject that wasn't taught internally at the school, meant that she could concentrate on those that she felt comfortable with; in fact, she sometimes still spoke French at home when Dad and Yetunde were reminiscing about the past. She had chosen well.

There would be whole school assemblies every other week, and today was a hastily convened assembly with an assertion that everyone had to be there. Mr Roderick, a physics teacher and football coach of the senior school team, welcomed her with an arm around the shoulder as she walked into the hall.

"The World Cup squad announcement becomes public at 9 a.m.," said Mr Roderick. "Our media sources have indicated that there might be a name from the school on that list."

Abebi felt shy, and a little guilty about not telling anyone.

"Right," she said with no particular inflexion to suggest what she meant.

"We are going to have a special assembly for you," he continued. "With the announcement being televised."

Abebi thought for a moment. "I'm not sure if they actually read out the names," she said. "I think it's just a preliminary list of names that gets published and then the coach is interviewed. At least that's what I'm expecting."

"That's okay," said Mr Roderick. "The media studies students have put something together this morning. We'll interrupt the assembly at 9 a.m. and play the message. We're all excited for you."

Abebi tried not to visibly cringe, but knew it was a big moment for the school. Students started to file into the hall, taking their usual spots by year and then by form. Abebi was directed over to where she would normally sit, but Mr Roderick positioned her this time at the first seat on the aisle. He smiled and left her there as more and more people poured in. Josie spotted her across the aisle.

"Hey, Baby," she said, surprised that she was on the aisle and not in her usual spot at the other end with the stragglers. "Are you excited?"

Abebi smiled. She had no idea what Josie knew. They had been firm friends since the start of school, had become teammates at Salisbury and were now at Adelaide United together. Their friendship was different now that they saw each other all the time, and they both accepted the fact that they should be looking elsewhere for friendship at school. Just as well that they weren't in the same form, but they were very close, almost like family.

Abebi guessed that Josie was referring to the squad announcement rather than the horrific circus of an assembly that was about to unfold.

"So nervous," she lied. She pulled a nervous face then they both cracked a smile as if they both knew.

"We interrupt this assembly," came a voice over the P.A. system lifted from an old movie. "We have an important announcement."

Music filled the hall, startling the audience from its slumbers—the subject matter of the assembly had been low quality, like a slow day on ABC News. The projector screen came down and the lights dimmed. Chairs shuffled, the murmuring started; this had everyone's attention.

"We now cross to Football Australia HQ for the announcement of the 2023 FIFA Women's World Cup squad."

Abebi could feel her phone buzzing erratically in her pocket. The announcement must have just been made public, but as far as anyone in the hall knew, this was happening live.

The names of the players alongside their squad number, their club and their club of origin scrolled up the screen as a voice not too dissimilar to coach Bernie read through the names. She would have been convinced it was her if it wasn't for a couple of stumbles and slight mispronunciations. The scrolling squad numbers reached the 20s and then number 26, Abebi Ngom, Adelaide United, Salisbury Inter (SA) appeared in a slightly different colour and then stopped in the middle of the screen.

There was cheering. It was canned cheering, but it morphed into the whole hall going crazy. The scrolling continued with the last few names as the spotlight shone on Abebi. At least there weren't any flashing lights and music.

"Come on up to the stage, Abebi Ngom, Australia's number 26!"

The hall was going off, everyone was on their feet, the high-pitched roar went on until Abebi joined Mr Roderick on the stage. As the crowd subsided a little, he spoke.

"We salute our newest sporting hero, Abebi Ngom, left-sided player with Adelaide United, star of the National Premier League with Salisbury Inter and the newest Matildas squad member for the Women's World Cup here in Australia."

Mr Roderick delivered it like a ringmaster, and the crowd lapped it up. Abebi hoped he wouldn't hold her arm up like a winning prize-fighter. He didn't get Abebi to speak, but asked the whole school to give her a round of applause, which of course they did. The lights came on as everyone was still clapping, and she had returned to her position in the Year 12 rows before the applause stopped. She was happy that her deep skin colour hid the obvious blushing that she was experiencing right now, but she was happy realising the lengths that the school had gone to to mark her personal milestone, and her heart was beating at double its normal rate.

Chapter 46

Selected

Ten days later the final squad announcement was made. Adelaide had endured some horrible weather, and the Salisbury Under 18s game was cancelled, but training had gone ahead both weeks and Abebi was called into the reserve grade squad to cover for some injuries. Being in the Salisbury senior set-up was almost as exciting as getting the Matildas call-up, although she sensed that she may have been called up as a PR manoeuvre by the club to show that they knew how to identify talent and provide a pathway to the seniors.

A new WhatsApp group had popped up on her phone the week before for the preliminary squad, and there were daily updates on the movements of the squad, almost like a newsfeed of what all the players were doing in the lead-up to the World Cup. With the A-League having ended some time ago, the European leagues having culminated in some success for the Matildas players, that left the US-based duo of Jasmin Calloway and goalkeeper Lisa Pirelli still in action, and the group included updates on their final games before they headed to Australia. Abebi left a comment on the group congratulating Jasmin on her starring performance, and the comment was quickly deleted. This was a one-sided group that was for information only, and Abebi felt silly for assuming she could use it to comment. She knew she had a long way to go to understand how everything worked with the Matildas and Football Australia, but she was very keen to try.

Abebi had been playing with her phone at the dining table for about an hour, trying to work out the features of her old but new iPhone, the one Josie had given her after she had upgraded hers to the latest and greatest edition. Messages popped up continuously to the extent that she swiped them off the screen without really checking what they were. One did pop up though from Bernie, asking Abebi to call her as soon as she could. Abebi was straight on to it, calling over Charles who was patching up a hole in the ceiling caused by the heavy rain recently. She sat up straight in her seat and ran her fingers through her hair to get it out of her face. Charles knew what to do. He got his mobile phone out, a battered oversized Samsung, and started to record as Abebi worked out how to put her phone on speaker.

"Thanks for calling," said Bernie. "I thought I wouldn't be able to catch you."

Abebi almost froze, hoping that she hadn't simply swiped away a previous message.

"Hi, Bernie," she stuttered. "What can I do for you?"

"I hope you've been waiting for this call," said Bernie, almost nervously. The shakiness in her voice was uncharacteristic and Abebi feared the worst. "I'd like to let you know that you have been selected in the squad of 23 for the 2023 FIFA World Cup in July. Welcome to the team."

There was silence. Abebi stared at Charles for a split second and her eyes were unblinking. Her face then broke into a disbelieving smile, a laugh that usually preceded tears, and her dad let out a whoop that brought Yetunde running from the bedroom. The phone call was secondary as Charles hugged his daughter and Yetunde took his phone to continue capturing the moment.

"I don't know what to say," said Abebi slowly, before blurting out, "Thank you, thank you, oh my god, this is incredible. Thank you."

She had tears in her eyes, not uncontrollable tears, but those of relief and she looked to the ceiling as if to seek validation from her mum. Yetunde kept recording despite drops rolling down her own cheeks.

"I take it from your reaction," said Bernie after a long pause, "that you will be accepting your place in the squad? As you know, the left side of our defence is a problem position, and you have a long way to go to be the finished product, but opportunity has knocked and this could be your big chance to break through. Are you ready to take the challenge?"

This was quite brutal by Bernie, and was the way that she was known to speak. She was pretty much saying that there was no other cover for the left side of defence and that she would only be given a chance if Daniella Gauchan were unavailable at any point. Abebi was happy to take the opportunity, and who knows, anything could happen during tournament football, even a sending-off and a suspension.

"I'm in," said Abebi. "What happens now?"

Chapter 47

Grill

From that moment, Abebi's life was a whirlwind. There were online meetings, lengthy phone calls with the Football Australia media team so they could find out more about her. When they got hold of the footage of Abebi learning of her spot in the squad they were overjoyed—this was the content they needed! There were appearances on local and national radio to talk repeatedly about herself, almost an introduction into her life and how she had settled in Australia with her family. Abebi was immediately asked to withdraw from NPL fixtures, although she was allowed to train. In fact, Salisbury moved her into first team training for the week, where perhaps she could learn more about the physicality required to play senior NPL football, and the Football Australia coaching team more or less told their contemporaries at Salisbury that she should be training at the highest level possible.

The new WhatsApp group for the full Matildas squad and a series of online meetings brought Abebi and her teammates up to speed with what was happening for the World Cup. It was such a thrill to hear the plans for a pre-tournament camp in Canberra with the majority of the squad, and then the entire squad would travel to the UAE and then on to Vietnam to play in two Asian Cup qualifiers that had, unbelievably, been scheduled just before the start of the World Cup.

And of course there was still her normal life that continued; frustratingly she missed out on her Under 18s fixtures and then she was asked to miss the final week of training before she headed to Canberra.

Even at school, her teachers, and especially Josie, prevented her from joining in football games at recess and lunch, even though interest in football was booming as a result of the scarcity of tickets. When she left school on the Friday, after only a week back following the school holidays, her classmates applauded her out of the door. Abebi felt as though she was leaving for good, and in a way she was; when she returned from the World Cup, life would surely have changed forever.

Yetunde waltzed through the door close to 7 p.m. Her scowl turned into a smile when she saw her sister standing in her Matildas tracksuit making final adjustments to her luggage. Abebi looked so professional, so grown up. She looked like a woman.

"Where have you been?" asked Abebi, in a tone that showed interest rather than investigation.

"Just hanging about with the gang," came the non-descriptive response. The gang? Hanging around? Abebi didn't have the capacity to take on the role of inquisitive mother just now.

Charles was serving up dinner, having obviously received a tip-off from Yetunde that she was close.

"What do you get up to between school and home?" he enquired, avoiding the steam coming from the rice cooker as he opened it. He had obviously sensed that this was a good time to ask, with Abebi soon to be away, and he perhaps wanted to let her know that she would be under watch while her big sister was absent.

"Oh, not much," she said dismissively. "Believe it or not, I did some homework at the library after school and then we hung around the shops for a while. There's not much happening around here for people like me."

She put her school bag on the table with a thump. They all looked at each other. Yetunde picked up her heavy bag again. There was an unease for a second as Yetunde raised her eyebrows.

"Sorry, we're eating here in a sec, I know, I know," she said, before disappearing into her room.

Abebi felt the urge to grill her little sister. She wanted to rifle through her school bag to see what was so heavy. She wanted to know what was going on inside her head.

"She's going to be okay," said Charles. "I've got eyes around the area. I would know if something was up."

"She needs a mother in her life," said Abebi.

"I can play that role too," said Charles.

"To the best of your ability, yes," said Abebi with a wise head on her shoulders. "But she just needs someone to guide her. I remember when I was 14. I didn't understand much, and I thought I knew everything."

Charles smiled. He would be thinking the same about Abebi right now, but masked it well, with a tender hug for his eldest daughter.

Chapter 48

Comportment

Arriving in camp in Canberra, after the shortest of flights from a stopover at Sydney airport to meet five other players and some staff members, the mood suggested a quiet determination in the group. The Institute of Sport was home for the next 12 days, and the first evening was spent getting a tour of the campus from one of the Canberra-based coaches who lived nearby. This was some sort of secret sporting wonderland, with so many top-class facilities, swimming pools, gyms, even a full-sized stadium and accommodation next door.

The players were assigned a roommate for the duration of the stay, Abebi twinned with an equally fresh youngster in Melbourne City's Mandy Uhlenstall, and they hit it off instantly. She wondered if there was some sort of *Married at First Sight* psychology that went on in pairing up the players. If there was, they'd got it right, and they sat up talking for a couple of hours before bed that night, getting to know each other and sharing stories of how they found out they were in the squad.

Abebi was enamoured by the whole experience in Canberra. The squad was initially made up of the Australia-based players, but over the two weeks, more players arrived from around the world. She had wondered why they were in camp for so long before the World Cup, especially when not all of the players were there, but after the first two days, she understood. This was intense. The physio team, led by the legendary Matildas player Nina Josifoski, spent so much time with the players that they got to know them really well. Their ability to eke out knowledge about past injuries was eye-opening; Abebi's ACL injury was at the top of the list, but by the time they had worked her body and concentrated on each part of the body in turn, they unveiled a weakness in her right shoulder and a slight misalignment with her posture. She even remembered getting her toes trod on in a game when she was in the Under 14s, which really hurt and turned her two end toenails black. A check suggested that the little toe on her right foot had in fact been broken and hadn't healed properly. It was like a competition between the players to get the longest rap sheet.

The arrival of the Swedish squad on campus changed the mood, combined with the appearance of the remaining US-based players, and the players were quickly reminded why they were there. The Swedish players were generally taller, with broader shoulders and they looked magnificent athletes; they had a chance to mingle with the Swedish players and staff and they all spoke impeccable English. Every one of them seemed to be addicted to coffee. This was one thing that made Abebi feel younger than the rest of her squad. Even the Matildas players, all clean-living, top-level athletes, seemed to have coffee at the top of their thoughts every morning, and were like newborn kittens crowded around the mother's teat of a coffee machine before they could function properly in the morning. Abebi had never liked coffee. She had it in the same column as wine; one day she would like it, but up until now, every time she had tasted it, her contorted face was enough to put her off taking another mouthful.

In between morning and afternoon training, which varied from light recovery-style sessions to heavy-duty fitness bootcamps, Abebi and a few of the younger Australia-based players were given over an hour of media training every day. It was a lot of fun, doing mock interviews, learning of the things not to say, preparing for the questioning techniques that would come their way when the interviewer wanted to know something specific. She learned to pause before she answered a question, just to give her a moment to assess what she was going to say, and that was quite a challenge as she had always previously spoken immediately after being asked a question, formulating her response as she went.

There was even a session on comportment, as they called it—how to stand, how to sit, how to maintain eye contact and posture. Mandy was really good at it, she seemed to have the straightest back while still looking relaxed, and Abebi tried to copy her. Being tall, she found it challenging, and she was warned about her natural stoop and how to correct it. The well-spoken middle-aged lady who joined that session, who seemed to be the oracle on the subject, made a comment at the end of the session.

"Abebi, you are the most striking, beautiful girl I have seen in a long time," she said. "You could be a supermodel."

Abebi could feel herself going red as the rest of the group looked on with joy and amazement.

"But you must stand upright," she continued. "You must enjoy your height. You must fill your frame; if you do that, you will look and feel so much more powerful in yourself."

That was quite a revelation. She knew that she had a tendency to curl up when she was uncomfortable; she often stooped unnecessarily when walking through doorways, but when she was on the football field, she felt that she was as tall and powerful as anyone else. She took the constructive criticism on board, though, and Mandy gave her a nudge and a hard stare the next time she found herself slumping her shoulders.

Some of the players had a photo shoot to model the World Cup kits, and Abebi was amazed that she was chosen to be part of it, especially after being critiqued for her posture. Helen Maxstead picked up the link between the players chosen, though, and it was clear that they were the multi-cultural in the squad. Vic Younis was of Turkish descent while Helen's ginger hair, bottle-white skin and freckles were striking. Lisa Pirelli, the goalkeeper, had more than a hint of Italian in her, and Anna Black was the petite English-looking girl. Add Abebi's dark skin and long black hair, and you had a real cultural melting pot. The group was having a laugh about it, teasing the main photographer, Nico, who was getting a little flustered.

"Will you have to dim the lights for my skin?" said Helen.

"Better not have a dark background," quipped Abebi.

"Should I have brought my *sheesha*?" asked Vic.

They were having fun. Nico was agitated, and tried to maintain his professionalism, but smiled when they organised themselves into a group shot and nailed it. A handful of Swedish players walked in as they were starting to get into the swing of it, clad in their blue change kit, and they had a similar cross-section of players, as much as you can with a squad made up of mainly six-foot, blonde-haired figures. After a moment, they were invited into the shot and asked to pair up with a Matildas player. Annalise Wallin, the powerful central defender moved in next to Abebi. Abebi was tall, but this girl was big and tall and could have wrapped Abebi completely with her huge arms. Nico organised them into various poses. Abebi caught Anna and her similarly petite partner Elin Berglund staring at each other and sensed some electricity. Anna looked at her feet for a second when she realised she was reddening in the cheeks and Abebi caught her eye with a smile.

The players were given a chance to see some of the photos on the screen of the camera, and they were incredible. It was magazine shoot quality, like the front cover of one of the glossy magazines her mum would bring home from work when the girls were younger.

Danni Marchese, the Football Australia photographer who had been snapping from the moment they arrived, rounded up the group and reminded them they had training in a few minutes, and they all took off. Danni captured their swift exit on camera, Vic running into the door frame and stumbling in laughter, a sure-fire entrant onto the outtakes on Danni's reel.

Chapter 49

Underwhelming

When the players had to leave camp for their Asian Cup qualifiers, Abebi felt as though she were leaving home. The two catering guys, who had looked after them for over two weeks with incredible meals, waved them off and the players all crowded at the windows to wave back. She wasn't the only one feeling sad to be leaving.

After an unimpressive victory against a weak UAE side, where Abebi came on for the final half an hour into a misfiring team for a thoroughly underwhelming full Australia debut, the Matildas turned on the style in Ho Chi Minh City when they absolutely bossed the much stronger Vietnam team and coach Bernie was glowing in her praise on the TV coverage. Abebi had warmed up at one point when Daniella Gauchan slid into the advertising hoardings on the sideline, but the left-sided defender seemed to be made of steel and was straight back on her feet and lunging into the next tackle once she'd been repaired by the physio team.

Coming onto the field in the heat of Dubai for her first Matildas appearance had been surreal. With only a small crowd to see it, and the game on during the night back in Australia, it would have gone largely unnoticed. Abebi though was walking on cloud nine that night, and cried when she was presented with a real baggy green cap by Daniella at the late dinner afterwards. There was barely any time to sleep, with the coach leaving at 5 a.m. for the airport the following day, but Abebi had called home to share her happiness and the sound of her sister's voice had her in tears again.

The flight back into Sydney was the most luxurious she had ever been on. The squad had the whole of business class on the Qantas plane all to themselves and it was like a party for the first two hours, until they reached the self-imposed curfew and the lights dimmed ready for sleep. Things were somehow very different when they arrived in Sydney. There were billboards and posters at every turn in the airport, and the squad was ushered into a special area just as the other people in the arrivals hall realised that they were in the presence of Australian sporting royalty. The option of a two-day break had been offered to the players, and half of them had taken up the offer, including Abebi. She was keen to get back to Adelaide to see her family, and if she was honest, she was in need of a break from the unrelenting intensity of the Matildas machine.

Abebi gave out hugs as she left the rest of the group to head to the domestic terminals, and again when they checked in at Terminal 3 to go to their respective gates. For the first time in three weeks, Abebi was on her own. She had been spoon-fed everything in camp, she didn't have to worry about what to wear, what to eat or when to drink, and there was an element of relief to fill up her water bottle at the fountain by her gate and unwrap the Mars Bar she'd just bought at the newsagents. This would only be a short flight to Adelaide, and she had organised for her dad to pick her up. As the plane took off, with her spacious seat at the front of the plane, she was asleep in seconds.

Chapter 50

Funny

The brevity of the trip home was laid bare when the plane was held up at Adelaide airport while ground staff cleared the area of a sewage spillage; all passengers were told to take their seats again after the mad scramble to grab bags and the jostling for position at the doors. Abebi was surprised by the impatience of her fellow travellers, even those at the front of the plane. Hopefully this wouldn't be the scene once the World Cup started, when thousands of football fans would be taking multiple flights to follow their teams around the country.

Charles was there at the gate—he couldn't wait until she came out at the baggage reclaim, he wanted to be there as soon as she got off the plane. Abebi loved it. Yetunde wasn't there, but Charles explained that she was having a strop in the car.

"She's been acting a little bit funny," said Charles as they waited for the Football Australia-branded travel case to appear on the carousel. "Can you talk with her? Maybe leave it until tomorrow when you're at home alone together."

"Sure," said Abebi, happy to be resuming the big sister and surrogate mum role that had been missing for the past month. "Is she doing okay at school?"

"Yes, yes," said Charles. "Her teachers were singing her praises at the parent-teacher interviews before the holidays. She just seems a little distant."

They were standing side by side as people pushed in front of them to get prime position for their suitcases. She put her arm around her dad's shoulder, which ended in a full-on hug. Her dad's body was jolting.

"I don't want to lose both of my daughters," he said into her jacket, pulling his head back when he noticed he was leaving tearstains on the blue fabric. "It's been so quiet without you here."

"Awww, Dad," was all that Abebi could muster. She hadn't left home, she'd just been away for a few weeks, but it had obviously had an impact on her dad. They were standing side by side again, and Charles put his head on her shoulder, recognition that she was now much taller than her father.

"I'll talk to her."

Charles left early for work, popping his head in to the girls' room as he always did to make sure they were awake. Except it was school holidays and he didn't need to, but he just wanted to see his girls before he left for the day. He walked out and closed the door, whistling a merry tune, and Abebi heard the car pull away after reversing from the driveway.

Abebi looked at Yetunde. She was so still, sleeping, the covers rising and falling with every breath. The Matildas' physio team had asked Abebi to get up by 7 a.m. today so she could get back into the right time zone, and she quietly got up, the clock reading 06:42 and the day just starting to break, the birds in full voice. She put away the dishes that were stacked next to the sink, trying her best to be quiet, and popped some toast into the four-slice toaster that she had bought just before leaving for camp. The old trick of frying bacon on the cooktop stirred Yetunde and Abebi had enough for them both, and Yetunde appeared around the corner looking a little dishevelled, but fully dressed.

"Hey," said Abebi. She hadn't quite worked out if whatever was bothering Yetunde was something to do with her. She hadn't said much at dinner last night, and Abebi was guilty for having held court, with Dad her willing interviewer.

"Hey," was the quiet reply, her gaze diverted as soon as Abebi looked at her. "You got enough for me?"

"Of course," said Abebi, shovelling bacon onto a piece of toast on a second plate along with some slices of rockmelon, kiwifruit and strawberries. She was breaking all the nutrition rules here, but it looked so healthy and so colourful.

"Grab some weapons," said Abebi, which startled Yetunde, before she opened the cutlery drawer to find two sharp knives and two matching forks. They both sat down at the dining table, before Abebi leapt up again to fill up two glasses with water from the tap.

"How are you?" she continued, expecting her little sister to be low on conversation. "Everything okay at school?"

It was like pulling teeth. Yetunde had one-word answers, but she asked Abebi plenty of questions, seemingly to deflect the limelight back on her. Abebi could sense it. The half-eaten slice of bacon on her plate told a story.

"What's wrong?" she asked.

"What do you mean?" asked Yetunde, looking deep into Abebi's eyes after a long pause.

"Something is bothering you. I can sense it."

"Come into the bedroom."

Abebi was taken aback, but did what she was told, and followed her sister into the bedroom. Thoughts raced through her head. All of them bad, and her curiosity was piqued. Yetunde went into the free-standing wardrobe and moved some bags at the bottom, producing a parcel, something wrapped in cloth. She unwrapped it slightly and pulled out a pistol. She held it in the palm of her hand. It was quite big and all of Abebi's senses heightened. This was serious.

"An eye for an eye," said Yetunde calmly, looking at Abebi intently, as if seeking her approval. "This is for Darius 'Bomber' Jensen."

Abebi could feel herself almost standing on her tiptoes. She couldn't breathe for a second or two. Her first intuition was to get as far away from this scene as possible, but her first reaction was to pick up the gun slowly from her sister's hand and examine it, like she would with a football boot when she went shopping at Rebel Sport in the city. Smith & Wesson was written on the side, as she turned it over and moved it around in the light. A registration number was engraved in the handle. This was obviously not Yetunde's. Abebi couldn't think of anything to say. She just wanted to take the gun and run.

"Is this real?" was the first thing that came out of her mouth. She spoke quietly. This was incredibly illegal and the thought of anyone in the vicinity of the house being able to hear her through the window kept her voice from getting raised.

"It's real," said Yetunde, pulling out a box from the cloth wrapping and showing her that it contained bullets.

"But what are you going to do?" asked Abebi, trying not to strain her voice and trying not to grit her teeth. She gave the gun carefully back to Yetunde. As far as Abebi was concerned, any false move could set the gun off and she didn't want it anywhere near her.

"I'm going to teach that bastard a lesson," said Yetunde with a scowl, almost spitting as she uttered the 'b' in bastard.

Before she could grab the handle and show Abebi what she planned to do, there was a loud knocking at the door and a cheery "Cooeee!"

The girls were spooked. Yetunde quickly wrapped the pistol back in the cloth and made for the wardrobe as Abebi flustered for a second and slid out of the bedroom, cursing under her breath, to go and answer the door. She knew it was Kath from two doors up; that was her signature call, but the timing was so, so poor.

"Oh, hiya, 'Bebi," she said as Abebi opened the door in a hurry. Kath was a voluptuous Indian lady who was the local expert on all things food, and she had half a tray of ripe tomatoes in her hands. "Charles out already? I promised him these beautiful tomatoes. All plump and juicy."

Abebi's eyes were wide as they scanned past her ample frame to the tray of ripe tomatoes. The way her brain was working right now, she had her dad and Kath in a sordid relationship, with the added bonus of free produce from her garden.

"Oh … thanks," said Abebi with a smile. Kath was not one to leave without a chat, even though Abebi was keen to close the door.

"We watched the game on the TV the other night," she said. "Oh, it was marvellous. We wish we could have got tickets to the games here in Adelaide, but we were too slow. That Lisa Pirelli is a good goalkeeper, isn't she? How was your trip? Sorry, I've not caught you in the middle of something, have I?"

"No … no, no," said Abebi, snapping out of her thoughts. "Do I take the tomatoes?"

Kath handed over the tray. She stood there as Abebi wondered what to do.

"Thanks, Kath, can't wait to see what Dad cooks up with these."

"Oh, there's enough to make a lot of sauce there."

"I bet there is."

"I'll pop in later when Charlie boy is home."

"Okay, thanks …"

Abebi closed the door as slowly as she could in her haste, glanced a worried look at the photo of her mum by the door and launched the tray onto the dining table as she raced to the bedroom and cursed when she saw that Yetunde wasn't there.

"Shit!" she exclaimed, opening the wardrobe and fossicking under the bags to find no sign of the cloth-wrapped parcel. She did a double-take when she spotted her battered old football cards wrapped in hair ties at the bottom of the wardrobe, the photo of Bolton Wanderers star Jay-Jay Okocha smiling at her. For a split second her mind was distracted.

"'Tunde! 'Tunde!" she shouted, but she knew she had gone, and the dark footprints in the dew on the patch of grass near the fence in the back garden told the story. There were many footprints by the fence. She had scaled the fence and was away.

"Oh god," said Abebi. "Oh god."

She was frantic. She grabbed her phone, but she didn't know what to do with it. She couldn't call Charles, could she? Who could she call? She needed to get dressed. She needed to be dressed in something non-branded. This was definitely not Football Australia business, and she had to rifle through her clothes drawers to find something that was warm enough but light enough to let her do a lot of running. She thought of ringing Josie, but swiped the number away. She had her dad's number up but cancelled the call before it started ringing. Then she ran out of the back door, with no plan, but a million thoughts running through her mind.

Chapter 51

Trigger

She raced to the main road, about a five-minute run at quite a pace. She was super fit, so it was a breeze. A bus was coming as she passed the first bus stop and she doubled back to flag it down. She half expected to see Yetunde on the bus, but she was nowhere to be seen. She cursed as she realised that the train was probably the quickest way to get to Adelaide; Yetunde would be miles ahead, especially with the traffic banking up at the roadworks coming into Salisbury. She knew she had to get to Magill. She remembered someone telling her that's where Darius Jensen, the man who killed her beloved mother Adenike, was now living. What she planned to do when she got there was anyone's guess. She hoped simply to catch up to her sister when she got there. For now though, this was a slow-motion pursuit that was tempered by the stop-sign-wielding workman, and she slumped in her seat and put her hands over her face. She couldn't be any further from the World Cup right now.

The bus blazed into the centre of Adelaide, as if the driver were in on the pursuit, but it was probably the fastest he had been able to drive all morning so he was revelling in the last few hundred metres of traffic-free road on King William Street. Abebi had been off her seat standing by the door for ages already, and she held on in terror as the bus zoomed up to the bus stop and screeched to a halt. The doors opened and she jumped the steps, making off in the direction of Currie Street and the buses heading east. Maybe she'd find Yetunde here, waiting for the same bus, but again, when she arrived at the bus stop there was no sign of her. At least there were a lot of people, which suggested there would be a bus coming soon.

She danced on the spot as the bus arrived. She had willed it to come quicker after spying it way down the street. She made sure she sat in an elevated part of the bus at the back so she could see out of each side. She would simply have to scan and hope to see her sister, in the hope that Darius Jensen's house was before Magill shops, her only point of reference in the area, and ultimately where she would get off the bus in pure hope. Abebi scanned and scanned, almost from when they hit Magill Road, and all hope was draining out of her with every bus stop.

All of a sudden, she spotted her sister. The distinctive two-tone beige and grey hoodie. The stooped walk with intent, the long legs, a plastic bag in her hand. Abebi pressed the button frantically to get off at the next stop. She trained her eyes on her sister, her head turning like a clown at the funfair, eyes wide and mouth open. She saw Yetunde veer slightly as if she were turning instead of crossing a side road, before a big truck got in the way. Again, Abebi was at the door of the bus well before it came to a halt and she launched herself through the doors even before they had opened fully, catching her shoulder with a big bang and almost turning her ankle as she landed.

She sprinted back down the road, and took a chance, crossing the road in between cars with blind optimism, her fledgling Matildas career flashing before her eyes as she contemplated having a sibling in jail for murder, and made it to the corner of the street where Yetunde may have turned. There was no sign of her up ahead, and she raced to the corner of the next street and glanced right as she crossed the road. She was sure she had seen Yetunde disappearing into a front yard, and she slowly made her way up the side road to where she thought she had seen her sister. There she was. Standing by the side door of an old brick house.

Abebi was frozen to the spot. Yetunde hadn't seen Abebi, but looked as if she was leaving for good. The cloth wrapping was on the ground, the gun was in her hand, the box of bullets making a bulge in her pocket. Before Abebi could regain composure, Yetunde had opened the door with purpose and walked into the house. Abebi scrambled over to the door and followed her in, her intuition telling her that she had to be there, and she was relying on her adrenaline to make the right decisions. She almost caught up with Yetunde as she pushed open a door that was slightly ajar, taking her into a bedroom. Abebi had just about caught up to her sister and saw the stunned Darius Jensen. It was definitely him. Tattoo on the back of his hand, slight scar under his eyebrow. He had headphones on and game controller in hand, sitting at a desk in wide-eyed confusion. He slowly took off his headphones and Yetunde immediately cracked the gun clumsily across the side of his head. As he regained his poise, she pointed the gun square in his face as he placed down his controller, a trickle of blood coming down the side of his face from a small but deep cut.

"Please, don't do this," he said, perhaps more calmly than Yetunde was hoping.

Yetunde pointed the gun closer. She was focused and still.

"You killed my mum," she said slowly.

Darius couldn't think of an answer to that statement.

"You killed our mum," said Abebi, walking up alongside her sister, who didn't flinch.

"Please, I beg you," said Darius. "This is a mistake."

The bedroom had posters on the wall of the Matildas, of Adelaide United, both men's and women's, and there was a photo of Abebi in amongst it too. Abebi noticed a member's lanyard hanging on a chair, and in amongst some papers, haphazardly arranged in an overflowing tray, she noticed a Bendigo Bank booklet. The blood emptied from Abebi's face. This was the benefactor who had paid for her surgery. Surely.

"'Tunde, don't do this. We can find a better way," said Abebi suddenly.

"Darius 'Bomber' Jensen," said Yetunde with the poise of a calm, cold-blooded killer, "this is for Mum."

Darius was staring at her pleadingly. He hadn't moved a muscle. Perhaps he was almost accepting his fate, perhaps he was trying to psych her out. Abebi's eyes were glued to her index finger, poised over the trigger. The end of her finger bent to touch the trigger and Abebi had to do something. She launched herself at the gun, pushing it and Yetunde's hand just as an ear-splitting bang filled the room. There was a smell of burning. Abebi expected to see Darius fall in a heap, but she saw that there was a lamp in a thousand pieces all over the bed and a black mark against the wall where the lamp had been.

Abebi stared at Yetunde. Yetunde still had her eyes trained on Darius. His face was ashen. He was shaking. She pointed the gun at his face again. All suggestion of resistance had drained from the strapping former pro-wrestler.

"Don't do it 'Tunde," said Abebi. "Let's get out of here."

There was a pause, a long moment when no one moved and nothing was said.

Yetunde looked ready to pull the trigger again and Abebi readied herself to dive at it again.

"Don't do it," repeated Abebi. "Don't ruin your life too."

After another short pause, Yetunde brought the gun even closer to Darius' face.

"If you say anything to anyone about this," she said through gritted teeth. "Anything! You are a dead man."

Darius nodded his head slowly, gulping as he did, still looking her in the eyes.

Abebi slowly took hold of Yetunde's elbow and moved the gun away from his face. She was conscious that any false move could lead to the gun going off again. Yetunde flicked on the safety latch, and seemed to snap out of the persona that she had been in. The two girls stared at each other, telepathically agreeing to flee. Yetunde took one step, then turned back, took aim and smacked Darius across the head again in the same spot. This time he was hurt, and fell off his chair onto the floor holding his head.

The girls scrambled to the door; Yetunde picked up the cloth wrapping and started to wrap up the gun, produced the plastic bag from her pocket and popped the parcel in. At least she was conscious about reusing a plastic bag, despite almost being a first-degree murderer. They skipped back to the street, making out that they were playing, laughing and joking to divert any suspicion. There were people in their front gardens and at their windows, looking further up the street for any sign of where the loud bang had come from.

"That was a loud noise, eh?" said Abebi to one of the old men at their front gates. "Do you know where it came from?"

"No, dear, it must have been further up the street," came the reply.

Abebi shrugged and walked off, followed by her innocent-looking sister, who skipped to catch up as they turned the corner. Then they ran. They ran back to the main road and turned right, back in the direction of the city centre, coming to a stop as a set of traffic lights allowed them to cross the busy road. As they were crossing, Abebi could feel herself getting angry.

"What were you thinking?" she said quietly.

"What do you mean?" said Yetunde.

"You were so close to murdering a man," said Abebi. "And where did you get the gun?"

"You don't need to know that."

"Do you realise how close you just came to changing our lives completely?"

"He deserves it."

"He's going to tell the police now."

"He won't."

"How do you know that?"

"He hasn't got the balls."

As they reached the other side of the road and broke into a jog to get to the bus stop before the approaching bus, Abebi had almost resigned herself to being embroiled in an attempted murder case; she felt that her big chance to play World Cup football in her own country was just about to be whipped away from her. She wanted to do the right thing and tell someone. She also knew that she wanted to play football for Australia. This had to stay quiet. They still had the gun. There was a 50/50 chance that Darius 'Bomber' Jensen would go straight to the police and they would be in deep, deep trouble.

They got on the bus, which was quite busy, and sat in silence all the way to the city centre. They changed to the train. Coming back a different way made Abebi feel like she was covering her tracks. They waited some time for the next train and made their way to Elizabeth and then walked the rest of the way. There were no police sirens. Yet.

Chapter 52

Love-hearts

Despite heading directly back home, it was already nearly midday. Yetunde walked straight to their room, still carrying the plastic bag, and closed the door. She obviously didn't want to speak any more about it. Abebi leaned on the kitchen bench, staring out at the lawn where she had noticed her sister's footprints heading to the side fence that morning. It seemed like four days ago.

Abebi had a number of calls. She checked in first with the physio team; the remit had been to go for a three-kilometre walk today, and she felt that she had ticked that one off, but she was relieved not to be wearing her GPS tracker which would have revealed some extraordinary peaks in her heartbeat. She then checked in with Victor Cilantro, the Matildas team manager, and they discussed her return to Sydney tomorrow afternoon. It was so soon, but it had to be. The squad had to be all together well ahead of the first game; there was so much interest in the FIFA Women's World Cup, and even Abebi had not envisaged such a fanfare in the local and national media.

She had a check-in with Mal Tierney, Football Australia's media guru, who explained some of the upcoming media commitments, and he asked if she was available that evening. Abebi was in no frame of mind to be talking to anyone from the media, where any slip could be fatal, so made the quite valid excuse that she was at her sister's training that evening and then spending time with her family. Being in an interview may have also made her feel as if she were being interviewed by the police, and that association made her even more determined to make the excuse watertight.

Mal urged Abebi to log on to Instagram and share some of the content that had been suggested in the WhatsApp group, and she dutifully opened the Instagram app and was sucked immediately into a vortex of Matildas hype. It was fascinating. She saw the photos from the kit shoot where the Swedish players had joined them at the end, and they were absolutely stunning. Abebi hardly recognised herself. This striking figure in the photos had immaculate skin, curves in the right places, and stood with an impeccable posture. She was more than happy to like and share plenty of those, and then started to load up some of the images from WhatsApp that a lot of her teammates had already shared. The amount of love-hearts next to her posts was already in the hundreds by the time she'd moved on to her emails. There were official emails from Football Australia, there was documentation regarding insurance, accommodation and flight details from Victor, messages from Adelaide United, the usual barrage of emails from Salisbury Inter with details of the upcoming games, who was on fruit duty, what the starting line-ups were. The messages stretched back for two weeks, highlighting the lack of care that she now took of emails. Anything urgent or important was through WhatsApp, everything with forms to fill out or detailed itineraries were on email. It was mid-afternoon and Abebi hadn't moved from her position, leaning on the bench with her elbows getting red.

Yetunde appeared. She was dressed for training.

"Can you come with me to training?" she said, as though this morning had been some sort of dream.

"Sure," said Abebi. "Don't you usually hang out with your friends before training?"

Yetunde looked at Abebi incredulously.

"I've spent my afternoons in Magill for the last three months," she said, sharply.

"What?" said Abebi, rocking back again against the edge of the bench.

You heard me," said Yetunde. "Now let's not talk about that any more. I'd like you to come with me to training. It'll be dark soon and I'm not sure if I'm ready to be on my own just now."

Abebi forced a smile.

"Of course," said Abebi, feeling needed, and not just a little wary of her sister. Her mobile phone had eaten up her whole day, and she was ready to get out and enjoy the cool winter temperatures.

"What do I do with the … the package?" asked Yetunde.

"Nothing," said Abebi with assurance. "Just leave it where it's been for the last two months."

Abebi had played a card that she never thought she'd play. She had had no idea that her sister had a gun in the wardrobe, but she made out that she had known all along. In fact, she had noticed the bags having moved a while back and thought nothing of it. In retrospect, she should have acted upon her instincts and checked underneath to see what was there, but she must have been in a rush at that moment and forgot all about it. What she had done just now though was take a punt to make her little sister believe that she knew all along. It was a power play that could have backfired, but as she stared into Yetunde's eyes, she could see the fear and the look of someone who had just been rumbled.

Yetunde looked ready to crumble. Abebi stepped forward and hugged her before stepping back and patting her on the shoulders as if to say 'Right, let's go'. They headed to training, as they had done so many times in years gone by when Dad was at work, Abebi in her Salisbury Inter tracksuit to make her fit in when she got there. Dad would pick them up later and they'd have dinner at home.

Chapter 53

Inspector

Charles left the following morning, as he had done the day before, popping his head in to the girls' bedroom and seeing the same scene of Abebi wide awake and Yetunde hidden under the covers. He'd be home early to take Abebi to the airport, making sure that Abebi turned down the offer of a chauffeured car to the airport. Abebi blew Charles a kiss, and could hear him talking and giggling with Kath before he got in his car and reversed out of the driveway.

Before she knew it, she could hear the car pulling into the driveway and realised that she'd fallen back asleep. Dad was super early, she thought, but she sensed that it wasn't her dad by the heavier sound of the car door closing and the bigger strides of whoever was in front of the house. She thought about the package in the wardrobe. She quickly spun out of bed, feet on the floor, poised, waiting for the next move from the driveway. Her next move would be to Yetunde to wake her up.

There was a light knock on the door. Abebi bolted to Yetunde's bed and shook her shoulder. She was already awake. They were spooked. They looked at each other, frozen in time. The doorbell rang and she heard another car pull up outside. Their number was surely up.

"Hello?" came the deep voice. "Chief Inspector Markie, South Australia Police."

Abebi realised she was holding her breath and let out a sigh. She turned towards the bedroom door as Yetunde questioned her next move with her hands. Abebi simply nodded her head and moved into the kitchen and across to the front door. Before she got there, the door handle moved, and a jangle of keys saw the door open. Charles was there, looking flustered, but showing the Chief Inspector the way into the house.

"Thanks for the call, Chief Inspector," said Charles, ushering his guest inside.

"Ah, hello, there," said the policeman as he saw Abebi in the short hallway.

"Can you get 'Tunde please?" said Charles.

Abebi didn't say a word and walked towards the bedroom. Yetunde appeared before she got there, carrying the cloth parcel, and Charles asked them all to take a seat around the big dining table. Yetunde clunked the parcel on the table. The girls were both like flowers, yet to unfurl into the morning sun, and they both looked incredibly shy and vulnerable, sitting awkwardly in seats that they had been so comfortable in for years.

Charles offered them drinks; the inspector, an older gentleman with grey hair and a knowledgeable look, took him up on the offer of a water. Abebi sprang to her feet and reached into the top cupboard to fetch the water jug and filled it with water while Charles found four similar glasses. They sat back down and the inspector spoke.

"I apologise for bringing up painful memories from your past," he started. "We have come into some information that may allow us to make a conviction in the case of Adenike's … your mother's … passing."

Charles looked at his daughters, who were non-responsive, their body language as closed as it could possibly be.

"With your assistance, we are confident that justice will prevail and we will be able to convict the assailant with a manslaughter charge."

Abebi realised that this had nothing to do with yesterday, at least not directly, and she relaxed her shoulders and sat properly in her seat.

The natural warmth returned to her eyes, and the tight feeling in her chest started to fade.

"The tall blond man?" asked Abebi, in a way that hid the fact that the two sisters had been in his presence only 24 hours earlier.

"The tall blond man, yes," said the inspector. "Darius Jensen. I'm sorry if that name is not one that you like to mention."

"What makes it different this time?" asked Abebi. Yetunde had shuffled in her seat once she had also realised that they were in the clear.

"We have a confession from Jensen himself," said the inspector. "He presented himself to a police station out east and asked if he could make a statement. The suggestion is that he wanted to come clean and set the record straight. Looked like he'd been in a fight."

Abebi and Yetunde looked at each other guiltily but with the suggestion of a smile.

"This *is* an interesting development," said Charles. "How would this play out? Would we need to go through a whole trial again?"

He was referring to the initial court case that was quite a circus, and where Abebi and Yetunde were required to give their version of events via video. It had been traumatic, and Charles was suggesting that he didn't want to go through that ordeal again.

"Not the whole trial," said the inspector. "The facts would not be in dispute. It would simply be a case of confirming the actual events, which I believe are exactly as Jensen described in his statement yesterday. We would be looking at a week in court at the most, and the majority of the previous evidence would simply be confirmed, including the video evidence of your two young daughters."

The inspector looked at Abebi and then at Yetunde, who were completely different people to the two fragile girls he had met only half an hour ago.

"... who are obviously not so young anymore," he said. That broke the ice. Yetunde beamed at him. Abebi looked at Charles who was looking lovingly at his smiling daughter.

"If we had to go through the same experience as last time, with all eyes on us and a whole load of lies from the defence, then I'd definitely say no, Chief Inspector," said Charles. "However, if you have a signed statement by that blond-haired bastard ..."

His demeanour had changed. Abebi and Yetunde were alarmed by the sudden change in mood. Yetunde's arm brushed against the cloth-wrapped package on the corner of the table. It was an involuntary twitch that she seemed to try to quell.

"... admitting his guilt and corroborating all of the witness statements," he continued, "then we will be in a position to put this whole horrible episode to rest, and we can have justice for my beautiful Adenike."

Yetunde grabbed his hand, Abebi put hers on their clasped hands. The pain was real.

Abebi slipped into surrogate mum mode, as she often did.

"Inspector, sorry, Chief Inspector," she said, correcting herself immediately, "we will let you know. Do you need an answer right now?"

"No, no," said Chief Inspector Markie. "We're ready when you're ready."

Charles had a devilish glint in his eye and the Chief Inspector gave a knowing look.

"Then, we will let you know when we're ready. It might not be for a few weeks," said Abebi. Charles and Yetunde knew exactly what she meant. She had a more pressing life event just about to start and she would need to be completely focused on it from this afternoon onwards.

Charles stood up, Chief Inspector Markie standing up almost at the same time, and they shook hands, with neither of them instigating the handshake.

"I'll be in touch," said the inspector, glancing at Yetunde and Abebi with an acknowledging nod. "Don't leave it too long."

Chapter 54

Rhythm

"You did what?" said Charles. He had promised not to get mad. The girls had decided to tell him everything, as soon as their dad had closed the door after seeing the Chief Inspector's car disappear around the corner.

"Dad, we're telling you this because you need to know," said Abebi. "I'm leaving this afternoon and you two need to be on the same page."

Charles looked at Yetunde, who raised her eyebrows and her head, unintentionally looking down her nose at him. She pushed the cloth bundle across the table so it was in front of all three of them and unwrapped it slowly. It turned out to be a big, dark-blue apron, and in the middle of it sat the Model 19 Smith and Wesson .38 pistol with a box of bullets that had one less than it did yesterday morning.

They sat and looked at it.

Yetunde picked up the gun in the palm of her hand, flicked a latch and pushed the barrel open with her two fingers, letting the unused bullets drop out. It looked as though she had done that same manoeuvre many times in the past, but she had forgotten to do it yesterday. She closed up the barrel, popped open the box and placed the bullets back in. There was a space for one more bullet.

"Do you want me to take this away?" asked Charles after a long pause.

Yetunde pushed the gun, which took the apron with it, in Charles' direction.

"Yes," she said. "I don't ever want to see that thing again."

Charles carefully wrapped up the gun and the box in the apron, in the same manner that he would have wrapped up a pair of shoes at his shop back home in Zambia. He stood up and disappeared through the kitchen to take the parcel out of sight. He reappeared half a minute later carrying a small box, maybe a jewellery box, and sat closer to Yetunde. He opened the box and sat it in front of her. It contained a ring, that when he pulled it out of the box, was attached to a necklace. He handed it to Yetunde.

"I want you to have this," he said. "It was your mum's engagement ring. I was going to give it to you on your 18th birthday. I think today is a more appropriate day to give it to you. I want your mum to be with you always. She needs to guide you in these difficult times. I can't always be here to show you what to do."

Yetunde bowed and put the necklace over her head. It squeezed on, just enough room to scrape past her ears. She took the ring in her hand and looked at her dad.

"And I want you to have this," he continued, looking at Abebi. He lifted the innards of the box and there was a second ring underneath, lying in the box. Abebi accepted the ring from her father and he prompted her to read the engraving inside. The light wasn't great and Abebi handed the ring to Yetunde, who had incredible eyesight.

"Adenike and Charles. Always together," she read.

"I know you can't wear it on the field or when you're training, but I want you to have it so you can always have a piece of your mum and me with you when you're not at home. I'm so proud of my daughters. You make good choices and you look after each other."

Abebi came around the table and they hugged together. It was a special moment, and there were tears, eventually turning to smiles when they started to reminisce about Mum. Abebi quickly grabbed her phone out of her pocket and brought up a song, an African beat filling the room and she started to dance the way her mum would have danced to the hypnotic music. Soon they were all up, shaking to the funky rhythm as if Adenike were in the room with them, Yetunde moving across to the door to dance in front of her photo.

Chapter 55

Icy

"Abebi, you're in our starting 11 tomorrow," said Bernie. Bernie had asked her for a quiet word as she walked into breakfast with Mandy. "As you know, Gauch is suspended, and I've thought about it, and I believe this could be your moment to shine."

Abebi was shaking. She thought she was cold, but Bernie's icy hands on hers, when her coach realised how nervous she was, confirmed that she was shaking in excitement.

The World Cup had already captured the imagination of the whole country. Despite a shaky start, the Matildas had come through the group stage and were now in the round of 16 against Sweden, their campmates from Canberra. It was a blockbuster game at the new Sydney Football Stadium, oddly named as Moore Park Stadium for FIFA purposes. It was Allianz Stadium as Australians knew it, and the winners would be most likely up against the powerhouse Germany team, who were playing some of the best football at the tournament.

Abebi tried to refocus and joined the dwindling line for breakfast, loading up her plate and arranging everything in an Instagram-worthy first meal of the day. Mandy made room as she approached the long table, and Abebi lifted her leg over the bench and slid in between Mandy and Anna. They didn't ask what the talk was about, it just wasn't that sort of atmosphere; players were having meetings and talks constantly, about tactics, about things happening at home while they were in camp, the coaches continually assessing the mental state of each and every one of their squad members.

The chatter at the table was about what they were all doing today. They had the day to themselves after a light session this morning, and before the 'minus one' training session at the venue of their Round of 16 encounter. Given the news she had received only minutes earlier, Abebi's ideal day would be spent doing nothing at all, mitigating the risk of injury; this was her big chance to play on the world stage, and she didn't want anything to go wrong. Mandy had suggested heading to Bondi Beach, but that seemed like a long way away, and Sydneysider Anna said that it might not be a relaxing way to enjoy Sydney.

Talk from the other end of the table was about taking a trip to climb the Sydney Harbour Bridge. There had been a block booking made by Football Australia for their out-of-town staff to enjoy the harbour's iconic bridge from the summit. A handful of players had already agreed to go and there were two spots available. Anna declined, as she'd already done it multiple times with overseas visitors when she lived in Sydney, but she assured everyone that it was well worth doing. The plan was set then, and Abebi and Mandy would take the final spaces, and that would be the ideal way to take their minds off the huge 24 hours ahead. The media team would be making the most of this opportunity, and team photographer Danni was already buzzing around at the other end of the table, asking who was joining them.

Chapter 56

Climb

As with anything that involved leaving camp, there was apprehension and heightened activity from team manager Victor, and he was camped out in the foyer of the hotel, making sure that plans were being followed and that the players who left were going to where they said they were going. He was like an exasperated dad at his daughter's 16th birthday party, trying to keep track of who's who. Security was tight, and they had the back section of the foyer to themselves, but once they were out into the main reception, they were out in the big wide world.

Abebi loved the fact that the minibus they were travelling in had tinted windows, and was relaxed, looking at the views of Sydney. There was very little to see at the beginning, the wide motorway taking them onto a very drab part of Sydney along Parramatta Road, but being out of peak traffic they made good time and coming around a bend, the harbour on the left, with the boats moored next to a rowing club and the floodlights of a suburban stadium overlooking the water, she had an idea of what the attraction was. The approach to the Harbour Bridge itself was slow, but the area it was in was like a throwback to the middle of last century, old buildings dominating, cobbled streets and stunning views of the harbour through the gaps in the buildings.

This was the best experience she'd had since being in Los Angeles for the friendly game with Mexico. The ceremony of donning the overalls for the climb was intriguing; it made the impending climb seem like it was going to be dirty and dangerous, but once out in the elements, and starting the climb, it wasn't even enough to get the heart going. What did get the adrenaline flowing was getting to the summit, and the Bridge Climb staff corralled them into position with the expert knowledge of Danni, and they made the most of their extended session at the very top of the bridge. They had photos from every angle, every photographer from the staff being deployed to get every possible shot of Australia's newest celebrities enjoying the view. Whilst it wasn't obvious where everything was on the horizon—no sign of Bondi Beach from up here—they spotted the Olympic Stadium where they were staying, way in the distance, and much closer in the opposite direction, they were excited to see Moore Park Stadium, right next to the Sydney Cricket Ground, two massive structures that seemed to be connected. It was wonderful. The harbour was sparkling. Sydney in winter wasn't a bad place to be.

The departure from the Harbour Bridge was swift—they were fortunate that the majority of people in the building were tourists with no idea who they were, and Danni was relieved not to see any journalists hanging around. They were back at the hotel next to Stadium Australia well before the 4 p.m. curfew, with time to change and be ready for their pre-training meal. As they exited the lift to the club floor lounge, Anna and Jasmin Calloway bounded out of the lift next to them, full of excitement as if they'd just stepped off a ride at the funfair. Everyone had obviously made the most of their day off in Sydney, and Jasmin quickly raced off to the bathroom when one of the chefs cheekily asked if she'd just been clubbing—Anna laughed that she'd had her makeup done in a department store in the city and she had forgotten all about it. Abebi was loving this; they were all on the biggest adventure of their lives.

Chapter 57

Congestion

Kick-off was delayed for a few minutes; apparently there was congestion outside and fans were struggling to get through the gates. The players were still in the changing rooms and Bernie had looked at her watch, wondering what was going on, the usual alarm not sounding and no official appearing at the door to hurry them up. It wasn't until assistant Ferdy Newton left the room and came back with the news that it all started to make sense.

"You see what this World Cup has done for football in Australia?" asked Bernie rhetorically. "People can't get enough of you. You are the reason why everyone is trying to get in to the stadium. You can rewrite history here. You can be the difference, the player who changes the way Australia and the world views women's football. Do you understand?"

There was no answer. All eyes were on Bernie for the next sentence, and it felt like every player was holding their breath. Before their head coach could rouse them even further, the pips came over the loud speaker, and the players stood up as one, Lleyton Hewitt *come-on*'s being hollered and studs being stamped on the floor in anticipation. Abebi was in amongst it, but was absolutely petrified. She had been to the bathroom multiple times and loaded up with water and sports drinks, and she genuinely felt light-headed. There was no way she was going to tell that to Nina as they lined up to walk out of the changing room to join their adversaries in the tunnel.

A signal from the match commissioner and a nod from the media operations manager and the referee began the march out to the field. Abebi was paired with a tiny girl as her mascot, and the fact that her mascot was also a bundle of nerves made Abebi feel relaxed, the assumption of mother role to this little six-year-old blondie making her swell with pride. Being in the starting line-up that lined up for the national anthems was new to her—she had done this a few times for grand finals and youth games, but standing there, facing the substitutes and all the staff, arms linked and smiling, this took it to a new level. With Sydney Olympics icon Nikki Webster starting the anthem just as the cheering died down after the Swedish anthem, Abebi could feel the words stuck in her throat. Here she was, an immigrant to the country who had only just received her first passport, singing the national anthem along with 50,000 others at the FIFA Women's World Cup. It was thrilling, and tears welled up in her eyes as the camera panned across the mainly stoic faces, and a teardrop rolled down her cheek as she sang '… in joyful strains …' with the camera fixed on her. That would be a moment preserved in time, a memento to the nation of just how emotions ran high for these short few weeks.

The handshakes done, and plenty of smiles with players that they knew really well from their time together in Canberra, and Abebi raced out into the middle of the Australian half of the field to savour the atmosphere. It was incredible. A small patch of Swedish fans at one end roared as the Swedish team reached them, but it wasn't easy to tell them apart from the rest of the fans, the predominant colour being yellow for both teams. The game kicked off to a crescendo of noise, and the Matildas were straight on the attack. Mandy raced down the left and her dangerous cross flashed across the face of goal with striker Pia Nicholls' outstretched foot a whisker away from raising the roof.

Abebi had little to do early on, but was busy, running lengths of the field from attack to defence and back again, overlapping with Mandy and covering when Mandy went on her exciting runs. Anna and Rhianna Geary almost forced an own goal as Valerie Lundin sliced another dangerous cross over her own bar. The crowd was at fever pitch. The expectation of the crowd was such that every time Sweden got the ball, a respectful quiet descended on the stadium, and seeing the Matildas dismantled by the much-fancied Swedes was not out of the realms of possibility.

Those fears grew when Elin Berglund sprinted away down the wing, Abebi having been drawn out wide leaving a gap, and the classy midfielder delivered a precision cross for Heidi Bengtsson to power a diving header past the despairing dive of Lisa Pirelli in the Australia goal. The Sweden fans were animated and noisy in the celebrations, but a roar started from the Matildas Active section, and soon the home fans drowned out the celebrations with shouts and cries of encouragement. A goal behind, this could have been the start of a slow capitulation, but Australia kept pressing. Abebi started the move that saw Joelle Martins jink into the box, step past the last defender, but her touch took her wide and she couldn't beat Ulrika Urvall at her near post. That moment had the fans off their seats and the half-time whistle was almost inaudible, the whole stadium singing 'Waltzing Matilda' and serenading the players down the tunnel.

Abebi felt disappointed. She had been out of position for the goal, and she felt that she hadn't been involved enough, almost a passenger.

"Keep going, Abebi," said Ferdy, grabbing her around the shoulder as they walked down the short tunnel. "It's going to come. We can't lose tonight. Have you heard the crowd?"

Abebi said nothing, but gave a nervous smile and marched to her spot in the changing room to grab her drink bottle. Bernie urged them to go for it in the second half, and there would be changes to deal with whatever game situations eventuated.

Chapter 58

Sweden

The second half was only a couple of minutes old when Anna went in for a crunching tackle with midfielder Berglund. The referee was quick on the scene, racing in as if she were going to brandish a card. This could be pivotal. The referee's mood quickly changed as she reached the two players on the floor, and Abebi could see that there were smiles and handshakes already. That could have changed everything.

Abebi was getting more of the ball now, the Matildas switching the play frequently and probing down the wings at every opportunity. A ball spilled out of a tackle, Shelley Prasad poking it back to Abebi in space. The firmly hit pass up the line for Mandy just evaded a Swedish foot and Mandy was off, racing up the left wing, every spectator rising off their seats as the Melbourne City winger sprinted to the byline. The cross was on for Pia in the middle, but Mandy picked a gap instead, pulling the ball back into a huge space in the middle of the park. Jasmin Calloway didn't need to adjust her stride and struck the shot cleanly, the ball arrowing up into the corner of the net past the full-length dive of Urval. What a goal! Abebi was never one for over-celebrating when a teammate scored, but this was something else. Jasmin had already leapt the advertising hoardings at the end and was being swamped by fans. Abebi raced over with the rest of the team and jumped into the scrum. The players were as happy as the fans, and the faces in the crowd were ecstatic.

When Shelley and Rhianna were substituted, Abebi was surprised and relieved. She had expected to be the first to be taken off, but with the scores level, there was no need for knee-jerk changes. Joelle came out wide, with Mandy moving to the right, and Australia had the momentum. No one was sitting on the bench. All the substitutes were standing and reacting to every kick and every tackle as if they were on the field. The atmosphere was breathtaking.

In almost an identical move, Abebi received a ball back from the midfield and played a first-time ball up the left for Joelle to sprint past her marker. She cut inside and delivered an exquisite cross-field ball to Mandy, advancing up the right. She looked to make the sprint for the byline, but instead cut in and fed the ball to Pia. Her deft ball back into the path of Mandy seemed to be done in slow motion, the defence flat-footed as Mandy ran on to the ball, and she took a touch before screwing the ball under the Swedish keeper and into the net for a brilliant second goal. Mandy was punching the corner flag by the time the rest of the players caught up to her, and she was knocked to the floor. Hopefully she would be okay under there, and by the time Abebi got there, all she could do was dive on top of the pile with no care for who was underneath or who would pile on top of her.

There was still plenty of time for an equaliser. Sweden poured forward. Lisa made a save at full-stretch to keep out a thunderbolt from Bengtsson, and with the clock paused at 90 minutes, Elin Berglund took on Abebi and got the better of her. As the diminutive midfielder shaped to shoot, Abebi launched herself in front of the shot, and her long leg blocked the strike, the ball looping out for a corner with the fans celebrating it like a goal. Sweden threw everyone forward for the corner, but Lisa got a hand to it and Yolanda sent it forward for Pia, in space on the right. Instead of running for goal she sprinted for the corner flag and stood waiting for players to arrive, the referee blowing the final whistle to avoid the potential for a full-on assault, and sending the crowd into a frenzy.

Abebi ran all the way to the corner flag with the rest of her teammates; Pia had dropped to her knees and the whole bench and all of her teammates raced to join her. She was on her feet by the time they started to arrive; it felt like a penalty shoot-out win. The players all celebrated together and then hugged one another, taking in the cheers from the crowd. They eventually retreated to the centre of the field, where Bernie gave the players the most uplifting speech and captain Helen Maxstead singled out certain players for praise. Abebi was amongst those names, that last-ditch tackle still fresh in the mind.

Chapter 59

Adoring

The players were hesitant about heading to the fans, with the knowledge that they would probably have a strict curfew, with plans already in motion for the quarter-finals, but Bernie and Ferdy sent them in all different directions to go and celebrate with their adoring public. Abebi knew where her dad and Yetunde were sitting, and went across to the bay. She heard Yetunde yelling furiously from a different section though and blindly made her way across, following the screams of "'Bebi, 'Bebi."

She spied her little sister who was bouncing and flailing her arms around and raced in for a hug. As she accepted Yetunde's exhausted body into her arms, she noticed more black faces around her, familiar faces that evoked memories of a crazy journey across the sea many years ago. They were all wearing the same shirt: white with a Pepsi-Cola emblem with Abebi Ngom replacing the name. She hugged Dad, who had the biggest grin on his face.

"You remember these faces, huh?" said Charles, pointing in the direction of Edouard and Marie. She recognised Marie, and couldn't believe her eyes. Her mind was still on the epic football game that had just happened, and her dad could have been presenting any old person to her and she would have hugged them. She did recognise the next person though—Aicha, who had been so kind to everyone on the trip over and when they stayed in the big house in the Northern Territory. Her sister Zara was next to her, and the thrill of the whole day got to Abebi, and she started to feel emotional. One of the three young soldiers who had almost messed everything up when they got to Australia wiped away a tear and Abebi noticed the t-shirts.

"What are these?" she said, turning Aicha around to see the back. It read 'Abebi Ngom, doing it for our sister' and Abebi was confused.

Charles whispered in her ear.

"Your Achilles operation …" was all he said. Abebi took a step back and her face dropped. The realisation caused her to lose concentration for a second as her mind raced. It had been a collective effort by family, a family she had forgotten she even had, that paved the way for her return to football. It was the reason she was here, right now, celebrating the Matildas' finest hour. So many questions swirled around her head. Yetunde came in for another hug and was laughing; Abebi remembered just how close they had come to changing their lives only a few short weeks ago. Abebi saw the figure of Mr Roderick, her school teacher, reaching in to stroke her head. This was mad. The group parted for a grinning Trent and Margot, all the way from Nhulunbuy, who hugged Abebi and Yetunde. Incredible!

Abebi was prised away by her captain Helen, who urged her to make the most of this moment. She was right,; she would catch up with her family and everyone else at some point in the near future, but for now, she had to capture this moment and soak in the most unbelievable atmosphere. This win was for the whole of Australia and she had to be part of the celebrations. The stadium was still quite full, at least in the bottom sections next to the field, and even the Swedish fans were making noise, serenading their gallant homeward-bound team with colourful songs.

Chapter 60

Mixed

There seemed to be a lot of activity in the mixed zone, the journalists all hanging around to catch the players as they filtered out of the changing rooms and onto the waiting bus. This was a first—it was usually empty at this point. Anna was hot property, but Abebi was collared by an African journalist for a few questions for the BBC, asking her how proud she was to be an African playing at the World Cup for Australia. She couldn't see the BBC logo without thinking of her dad's boot business. The next person in line was familiar, El Hadji Diouf, Senegal international, former Bolton Wanderers player and now journalist, who was surprised to be offered a hug. They talked about the good old days at Bolton, Abebi telling him whose name she had on her shirt, before they slipped back into professional mode for a swift two-question interview. That was a surreal moment! The rest of the journalists were scrambling for any words from the other players, and Anna was led through the pack by media man Mal, an unusual face at this part of the game day experience. Something was obviously going down, the media pack was rabid.

The bus was going crazy; Anna had just got on and 'Love Is In the Air' was playing on Jasmin's music box. Everyone was singing along. Abebi looked around and she was the last in the carpark and the bus was running and ready to leave. Mal asked her if everything was okay.

"I don't know, Mal," said Abebi truthfully. "I don't understand anything at the moment. Someone is going to have to sit me down and tell me all about it in the morning."

"Let's get some sleep tonight and catch up tomorrow," said Mal. "It's been a whirlwind for you, that's for sure."

The bus was quiet now, but she noticed a faint murmur of a song as she walked up the steps, the players all quietly chanting 'sha-la-la-la-la-la-laaaaah'. She recognised the song from the A-League. As she appeared at the top of the steps next to the driver, the whole bus got to their feet, chanting the same.

"Sha-la-la-la-la-la-lah. She is Abebi Ngom," they all shouted at the top of their lungs. "Sha-la-la-la-la-la-laaaaah, she is our number one!"

Abebi smiled. Her face was already aching from laughing so much in the changing room, and she walked down the aisle of the bus to high fives, hands on her shoulders and pats on her back. Australia were in the quarter-finals, Abebi had just played 90 minutes against one of Europe's strongest teams and the whole country was going crazy for their newest heroes: the Matildas.

Acknowledgements

Anyone who has written a book and had the fortune of having that book published understands the amount of time and effort that goes into the process. The editing, proofing, sensitivity reading, cover design, scheduling and publishing of a novel, in a space that is in no way guaranteed a return on investment, is a leap of faith that never ceases to amaze me. Thanks to Bonita Mersiades for believing in my writing, and thanks to Fair Play Publishing for giving a voice to Australian football fiction writers.

A special shout-out to Blacktown City Under 20s Women's squad for giving me fuel for the football themes in this novel. Actively following the Matildas and Sydney FC Women, sometimes in a media context, has also given me more insight into how women's football works. It really is a fantastic environment to be around and I encourage everyone to get out and support their local A-League team. Thanks also to Nic for the initial review of the content from a completely different point of view.

If you haven't read *Anna Black - This Girl Can Play*, I encourage you to get your hands on a copy and relive the magic of the World Cup in 2023. A book conceived even before the host countries were announced, where the nation stopped for a glorious month of top-level women's football and the Matildas captured the hearts of the public, mirrored the joy and excitement conveyed in Anna Black. It's my Johnny Warren 'I Told You So' moment, and I am delighted that real life imitated fiction and we had that amazing tournament in our own country. You'll also find Abebi Ngom in that story too.

If you enjoyed this book, or if you have any feedback, please like, comment or share on social media. Look me up. Give me a reason to write the next one.

About the Author

Texi Smith is a football fiction writer, reporter, and photographer with *The Roar*, a Sydney-based online publication.

He is also an active supporter of the Matildas, the Socceroos, and Sydney FC and a lifelong fan of Newcastle United, having grown up in the northeast of England. He still plays in an Over 45s competition, referees in a local league, and has also previously coached and managed at club level.

Away from football, Texi has an IT consultancy and is a member of the Bridge Club - a group of runners who have run ten or more Sydney Marathons.

Abebi is Texi's sixth football novel, his previous five chronicling the careers of Jarrod Black and his sister, Anna Black.

MORE REALLY GOOD BOOKS FROM POPCORN PRESS

RIPPA!

The End of the Game

The Yawning Giant

High Heels and Low Blows

Captain Courageous

Jarrod Black Chasing Pack

Anna Black - This girl can play

ALSO FROM FAIR PLAY PUBLISHING

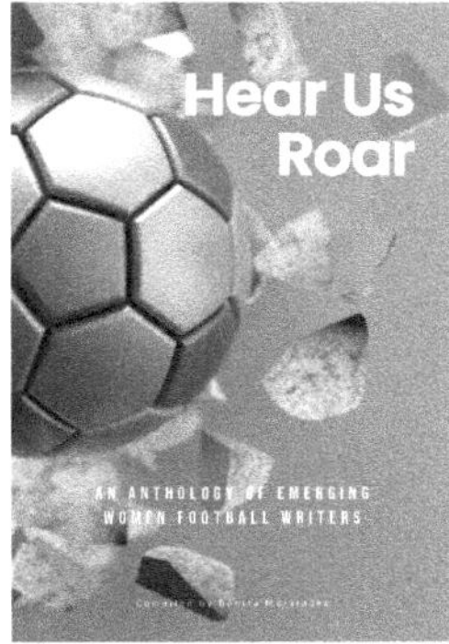

Hear Us Roar

"Get Your Tits Out for the Lads"

The Agents' Game

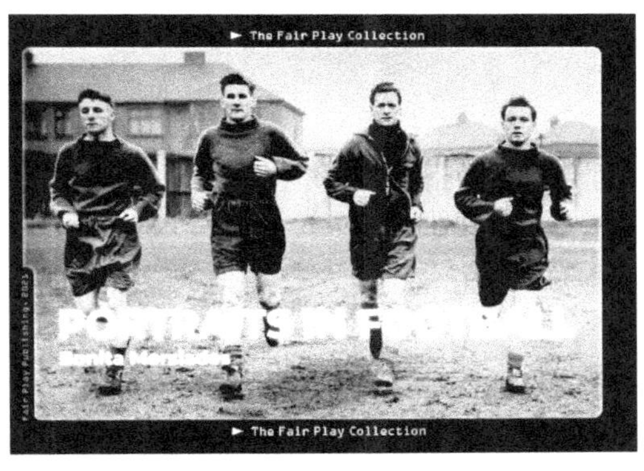

Portraits in Football

Turning the Tide

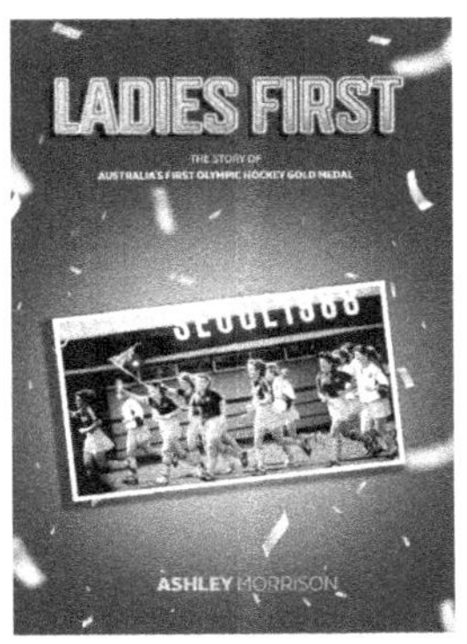

Ladies First